THE COMPANION AND THE EARL: A REGENCY ROMANCE

ROSE PEARSON

THE COMPANION AND THE EARL

Ladies on Their Own: Governesses and Companions

(Book 3)

By

Rose Pearson

© Copyright 2022 by Rose Pearson - All rights reserved.

In no way is it legal to reproduce, duplicate, or transmit any part of this document by either electronic means or in printed format. Recording of this publication is strictly prohibited and any storage of this document is not allowed unless with written permission from the publisher. All rights reserved.

Respective author owns all copyrights not held by the publisher.

THE COMPANION AND THE EARL

PROLOGUE

"Have no doubt, Miss Fullerton. *This* year, we will be successful."

Miss Deborah Fullerton tried to smile but her heart was so heavily weighted that it was a struggle to even attempt to do so.

"You do not have the same hope as I, I think." Lady Havisham turned her head and looked sharply back towards Deborah, who merely spread her hands. Lady Havisham sighed heavily and shook her head. "I can well understand such emotion my dear, for as you well know, I was once a companion also."

"Yes, I do recall you informing me of such a thing."

Deborah wanted to tell her employer that simply because *she* had found herself a rich and handsome husband despite being a companion, that did not mean that such a thing would occur for Deborah herself! She had not had any other choice but to become a companion and, given her lowly status, Deborah had very little hope that any gentleman would so much as glance at her. Lady Havisham, however, appeared to be more than a little determined that such a situation would take place and Deborah had no doubt that the lady would remain so determined for the entirety of the London Season. She had been so last Season also, when Deborah had accompanied her first to London and, thereafter, to a house party but, despite Lady Havisham's attempts to find Deborah a suitable match, there had been no success to speak of.

"You see, my dear, I have been considering your situation a great deal of late and have come up with the answer to all of your struggles!" Lady Havisham turned away from the window and walked across the room so that she might sit near Deborah. "I am sure that you will think me a little ridiculous, but once you consider it, I know that you will understand why I believe it to be such an excellent idea."

Deborah folded her hands in her lap and waited for Lady Havisham to continue.

I must be appreciative, no matter what it is she tells me.

After all, Deborah was well aware that she had been brought into the home of a very kind lady who did not treat Deborah as a hired companion, but rather as though she were a poor relative who required her assistance and guidance – and that was a very fortunate situation indeed.

"You will marry my son."

A gasp ripped from Deborah's lips; her outward calm composure gone in an instant.

"I know, you will think it quite a ridiculous scheme, but I believe that it would be an excellent match! My son has more than enough wealth for both of you *and,* since he is an Earl and you a Viscount's daughter, there can be nothing said about such a match! It would be more than appropriate." Smiling, Lady Havisham sat back a little more in her chair and tilted her head to the side a little. "What do you think, Miss Fullerton?"

Deborah struggled to answer. Her mouth moved but no sound came out, her throat tight and beginning to ache. The thought of marrying the Earl of Havisham was not one that she had *ever* considered, even though he was the son of her employer. Deborah had always considered herself to be far below such a gentleman and even the thought of presenting herself to him as an eligible young lady was a rather distressing one.

"You are overcome." Lady Havisham smiled, clearly quite satisfied with Deborah's response, and considering it – somehow – to be a positive one. "My son has his faults, however, so you may not find him *entirely* to your liking – but again, that is why such a match would be the most suitable of situations. Your gentleness, kindness, and sweet nature would remove his less than desirable qualities, making him the most excellent of gentlemen. I am certain that he would make you the very best of husbands."

Still, Deborah could not speak. She had never met the Earl of Havisham, having only taken up the position with his mother almost three years ago, and considered him, in her own mind, already to be rather selfish and prideful. In those years he had never once begged to visit his mother and certainly did not write to her regularly! Last Season, he had chosen to be in Bath when his mother had been in London, and when they had gone to Bath, they discovered that he had taken leave to London! Why would she ever think well of him now?

"My son need not know of my intentions, however, just as we hide all such things from your father." Lady Havisham shrugged one shoulder lightly. "When it all works out and he declares himself to be in love with you, *then* I may take a little pride in what I have arranged but, until then, he shall know nothing of it all."

A small band of relief wrapped around Deborah's chest.

"I see." Her voice was brittle and tight. "I am not sure, Lady Havisham, that I would be at all suitable for such a gentleman. You know that my father is impoverished due to his foolishness and that, therefore, I have had to become a companion. That in itself will push a good many gentlemen away from my company."

Lady Havisham tutted gently, her green eyes turning back to search Deborah's face.

"Ah but that is their own foolishness, Miss Fullerton," she answered softly. "They do not know your character and do not give themselves any occasion to even think of you in such a way! That will not be the case with my son for, given that we are to reside with him in London, he will have many opportunities to be in your company."

Her self-satisfied smile did not bring Deborah any sort of relief. Instead, questions began to pile up within her until she could not hold them back any longer.

"You speak of his household, Lady Havisham? Do you intend to reside with Lord Havisham? At his estate? Or in London?"

A gentle laugh broke from Lady Havisham's lips which unsettled Deborah even more.

"Goodness, you are eager! We are to go to London, Miss Fullerton, and shall arrive there within the fortnight. I have only just sent my son a letter informing him of this." Her lips twitched and a small line formed between her brows, her eyes becoming hard. "He will not be able to escape my company this Season, for I know that he is already in London and has no intention of making his way to Bath."

Deborah dropped her head but did not speak another word. Lady Havisham asked her to ring the bell for tea, and Deborah rose obediently, pulling the cord gently before meandering to the window and looking out across the estate lands. Lady Havisham had lived here for many years, ever since the death of her husband. It was traditional for unmarried gentlemen to permit their widowed mothers to continue to reside with them until such a time as the Dower House was prepared and they married, but Lady Havisham had eschewed such traditions and had made her way to the Dower House within the year of her mourning. Deborah thought it one of the most beautiful estates she had ever seen and had been glad to reside here, but now the thought of being pulled from it all and taken to London was quite upsetting. And for Lady Havisham to have the intention of marrying Deborah to her son made the situation all the more untenable!

"You need not be so concerned, my dear." Lady Havisham's voice floated towards Deborah, soft and filled with encouragement. "It will all come about as I have planned, I am certain of it."

Deborah turned her head and gave the lady a half-smile, whilst her heart began to sink all the lower in her chest. This was the most dreadful scheme, she was sure, but there was nothing for her to do but go along with Lady Havisham's intentions and wishes – no matter how discomfiting or frustrating such a situation might be.

I must hope that Lord Havisham is good-natured, she thought to herself, biting her lip. *Else things could become very difficult indeed.*

CHAPTER ONE

"You have a letter, my Lord."

Jonathan sighed and plucked it from the butler's fingers.

"Very good."

He dismissed the fellow with a wave of his fingers and then glanced towards his friend who seemed to be intent on drinking all of Jonathan's fine brandy, given that he was now on his third glass.

"Are you not going to read it?"

Lord Harrogate threw back the rest of his third glass and let out a long, contented sigh as Jonathan turned the letter over in his hand inspecting the seal.

Mother.

"Alas, it is not the letter I was hoping for," he told his friend, setting the letter down on the arm of the chair and watching as it slipped down in between the chair and the cushion. He did not reach for it. "This one is from my mother and does not merit any sort of swift reading or reply!" A stab of guilt followed his words, but Jonathan ignored it quickly. Even before the passing of his father,

Jonathan's mother had been eager in her attempts to get him to marry. Most of the young ladies she had suggested had been quite suitable, but had not been of any interest to Jonathan – mostly because he did not want to wed! Thus, he had been doing his best to avoid her company and for these last few years had succeeded rather nicely, although that did not come without a never-ending swell of guilt which seemed to grow with almost every day that passed.

"You were hoping for a letter from Lady Ensley, no doubt?"

Jonathan chuckled, then shook his head.

"Lady Ensley is not to be mentioned again, Harrogate," he warned, as his friend rolled his eyes. "It is not my fault that she did not declare herself to be wed before I began to pursue an... interest in her."

It had been a small, yet rather messy affair, but given that Jonathan had never intended it to be a connection of significance, it had not been particularly difficult to bring things to a close, especially when he had discovered that the lady was *not* widowed, as she had said.

"And is she returned to her husband?"

One shoulder lifted in a half-shrug.

"I presume so. As I have said, I have no interest nor connection with her any longer."

Lord Harrogate sighed and settled back a little more in his chair.

"She was a very beautiful lady."

"Indeed." Jonathan smiled to himself at the memory. "Alas, I shall not hear from her again. Instead, the letter I wish for is from my steward at the estate. I have written to request a statement about how things stand, especially with the crops."

"That is all very dull." Lord Harrogate yawned. "Your mother is not to stay at her own house, then?"

Again, Jonathan shrugged.

"I do not know. Nor do I care."

"Do you think she will take herself to Bath for this Season?"

Jonathan sighed, wanting to end the discussion about his mother just as soon as he could.

"I do not know. But I shall find out, no doubt." He gestured to the letter. "I am sure that she will inform me of precisely what it is that she intends to do this Season and I, in turn, shall plan to do the exact opposite." Grinning, he pushed himself to his feet and picked up his brandy decanter, pouring himself a second and Lord Harrogate a fourth measure. "If I am to have some time in Bath and then return to London, then so be it! Bath does not have all that London has to offer certainly, but it is quite delightful and has excellent company."

"And should she come to Bath?"

"Then I shall return here to London for when the Season begins properly in a few weeks hence," Jonathan declared, once again pushing away any niggle of conscience. "I have no doubt that, should my mother reside with me for even a few days, she would offer me at least three separate young ladies who, according to her sensibilities, I simply *must* meet." Rolling his eyes, he grinned at his friend's bark of laughter. "I, however, would find them all quite beautiful, quite lovely and yet entirely unremarkable. I would not wish to continue in their company and certainly would have no inclination towards furthering an acquaintance with them. This, in turn, would leave my mother frustrated and I equally irritated, given that I am not at all inclined towards marriage as yet."

"But does she not consider that?"

Jonathan sighed and passed a hand over his eyes, his smile fading. "My mother has always been of the mind that I should marry and marry soon. She, I believe, wed when both she and my most excellent father were a little later in years and that was something that she did not like."

"But she was still able to produce both yourself and your brother." Lord Harrogate arched one eyebrow. "Surely that is all that is required. When you wish it, marry a lady who is young enough to make certain that your family line is going to be continued."

Hesitating, Jonathan spread his hands.

"Certainly, that is a consideration."

He did not say anything more but reached for his brandy so that he might take another sip. On that point, Jonathan found himself a trifle more unsettled. He did not want to take a bride simply so that she might produce the 'heir and the spare' as so many put it. Nor did he wish to simply see his wife only on certain occasions whilst, in the meantime, maintaining entirely separate lives. Lord Harrogate might be contented with such a situation, but Jonathan knew that it would not suit him. He wanted very much to have a wife who would be something of a companion to him, to be there to converse with, to dine with, and to enjoy walks and carriage rides with. That was, perhaps, not what most gentlemen considered, but it was what Jonathan himself wanted – not that he shared such expectations and hopes with his friends for fear of mockery!

"You are not going to open the letter then and see when and where your mother is coming?" Lord Harrogate arched one eyebrow. "You will need to prepare yourself."

Jonathan waved a hand and threw back the rest of his brandy before he answered.

"I shall do so in time," he stated firmly. "There is no particular rush at present."

And thus, the conversation continued, with talk of balls, of soirees, and gossip that either had overheard and, of course, of the young ladies who were at present in London. The letter from Lady Havisham remained quite forgotten and, indeed, as the days went by, Jonathan did not recall that he had not opened it and quite forgot that he had received it at all. It sat in between the chair cushions, resting there, and allowing itself to be quite forgotten as the days drew on and Jonathan threw himself into London society.

∼

"My Lord?"

Jonathan groaned and did not lift his head from where he now rested it on his arms.

"I am certain, Armstrong, that I told you I was not to be disturbed this morning."

His butler cleared his throat.

"Indeed you did, my Lord, but there is such a happening taking place that I had no choice but to interrupt you."

His head felt so very heavy that Jonathan struggled to lift it.

"What is taking place?" he asked, his vision a little blurred still. "Is there something wrong?" A frown formed across his brow as he took in the way his butler shifted from foot to foot. "There has not been an accident?"

Shaking his head, the butler steepled his hands together, stilling completely.

"My Lord," he said, with as much calmness as he could.

"Your mother has arrived and insists that she is residing here for the Season."

In an instant, Jonathan became completely alert. His eyes flared and he looked directly back at his butler, who gave him only one small, rather solemn nod.

"Residing here?"

The butler spread his hands.

"We had no knowledge of this, my Lord. I can only apologize that we were not prepared."

Jonathan shook his head, flapping one hand towards the butler.

"There is no blame here, Armstrong. I did not know and thus, did not prepare you. I –"

He stuttered to a stop, his eyes flaring wide as he stared at the butler in slow growing horror.

The letter.

He had not read it. He had not even opened it and that, no doubt, was the reason for his shock at present. Lady Havisham would have informed him of her arrival in that particular letter, but he had quite forgotten about it. Closing his eyes, Jonathan dropped his head and groaned.

"My – my Lord?"

The butler sounded distinctly concerned and Jonathan could only shake his head, letting out a long, slow breath that did nothing to take away his frustration.

Planting both hands on his desk, Jonathan opened his eyes and muttered darkly under his breath. It seemed that he was going to be unable to escape from his mother this Season as he had done last year – and it had been all of his own fault.

"Have my mother's room prepared as quickly as possible." Straightening, he let out another frustrated sigh. "Ask her to wait in the drawing-room until such a time as her room is prepared and I shall join her there in a few minutes. Make sure there are refreshments sent up as soon as possible."

The butler nodded but did not turn away.

"And – for her companion, my Lord?"

Jonathan frowned.

"Companion?"

"Yes, my Lord. Lady Havisham has a companion by the name of Miss Fullerton. She also requires a room."

"Ah." Twisting his mouth to one side, Jonathan considered. He could not give her a servant's room, for the companion would be much above that. However, she was not as high in status as either himself or his mother so would not be placed near them either. He bit his lip. "The small bedchamber to the rear of the house would suit her very well."

The butler's brows flickered but he did not say anything, choosing only to nod.

"Is there something the matter?"

"No, my Lord. It is only that the green bedchamber – the one of which you speak – will require some hours of preparation. It is under dust covers and has not been used in some time."

Jonathan's frustration grew.

"That does not matter," he stated, unwilling to change his mind. "The companion will have to wait until it is prepared."

Inclining his head, the butler took his leave without another word, leaving Jonathan to wallow in his frustration and upset. Raking one hand through his hair, he let out a long, heavy breath and closed his eyes tightly again. *Why did I forget about that letter?* If he had read it, then he would have had time to make preparation to return to Bath and leave the townhouse ready for his mother. Now that she was here – and he also – there was no simple way to remove himself to Bath without his mother either insisting that she join him or heaping so much guilt upon him that he would decide, thereafter, not to go to Bath after all.

The entire Season now stretched out before him like a dull river, muddy and brown, whereas only a few minutes ago, he had seen it sparkling and bright. With his mother always watching him, always encouraging him to speak to one lady or the next, he would be troubled, frustrated, and irritated by her presence and her company – but he could do nothing about it now.

Taking in a deep breath, Jonathan lifted his chin and walked around his desk towards the door. He would have to make the best of it. Certainly, he could attempt to make sure that his mother was always distracted by some event or other and could be quite plain in his expectations but, even then, Jonathan was certain that she would continue as she had always done.

As he walked quickly to the drawing-room, Jonathan's heart sank lower with every step that he took. When it came time for him to step into the room, he paused, drawing in another long breath, setting his shoulders, and forcing a smile he did not truly feel to his lips.

And then he stepped inside.

"No, no, she is to go in the room next to my own." His mother was busy directing something towards the butler, who was standing with his hands clasped behind his back, nodding slowly. "That will do her very well. Ah, there you are! Come and greet your dear mother. It has been some time, has it not?"

Jonathan smiled and walked towards her, his hand outstretched to take hers. Pressing a kiss to it, he took his mother in. She was just as he remembered her – only half a head shorter than himself, with piercing green eyes and white hair which shone with strands of gold.

"It is good to see you, mother." A little surprised that the sentiment was quite true, Jonathan's smile grew. "It has indeed been some time."

"It has been near to three years, my dear boy." His mother's smile was fixed, her eyes a little sharp. "I was sorry not to see you last Season. Or at Christmas time. I had thought that you might come to visit for a short while."

"Alas, the roads were very bad, and I dared not attempt the journey." Jonathan put one hand to his heart, knowing full well that, whilst that was true, it had not been the reason for his absence. "But you had your companion, did you not?" He glanced about the room but did not see the lady. "I quite forget her name."

"Miss Fullerton." Lady Havisham's eyes were slightly narrowed now as if she had expected better of him. "You have not met her yet, as I recall."

Jonathan shook his head.

"No, I have not. But if she has brought you a little contentedness, then I am very happy to have you both here." That lie slipped easily through his lips, but his mother did not look convinced. Evidently, she knew him a little too well to accept such a thing without hesitation. Clearing his throat, Jonathan looked all around the room again. "And where is Miss Fullerton?"

"I have sent her to my bedchamber with my things and then she is to settle her own things in the blue room."

Frowning, Jonathan glanced sidelong at his butler who was standing with his hands clasped in front of him, his face impassive.

"Mother, I have told the butler to place Miss Fullerton

in the bedchamber at the back of the house. It is more than suitable for a companion."

"And I have told Armstrong not to be ridiculous," came the sharp reply. "That room is still under dustcovers, is it not? I recall it being so when I was here last Season. And since you *clearly* were not expecting my arrival, I assume that it is still in such a state? Whereas the blue bedchamber will only require a little dusting and clean sheets for the bed. Is that not so?"

Jonathan wanted to protest, but one look into his mother's face and he knew that it would be pointless. Perhaps it was that Miss Fullerton, being a little older, would require a room that was largely free of dust so that her lungs did not trouble her. Sighing, Jonathan threw up both hands and gave the butler a sharp nod. He departed quickly, leaving Jonathan and his mother alone.

"Shall we sit down?" Jonathan gestured to a comfortable chair by the fireplace, and Lady Havisham sat down quickly, sinking back with a soft smile on her face.

"It is pleasant to be comfortable once more. The carriage journey was rather arduous." She smiled at him. "Thankfully, I had Miss Fullerton to keep me company."

"That is good." Jonathan tried to picture the lady in his mind, considering her to be of an age with his mother. "And you have found her beneficial for you?"

"Indeed, she is quite lovely," came the reply. "A very kind lady, I must say. She is always thinking of others and wondering what she might do to please them. I have found her to be most generous in spirit."

"And what is her background?"

Lady Havisham smiled.

"She is the daughter of a Viscount."

"I see." Jonathan tilted his head, thinking that it must

have been very difficult for such a lady to have been forced into employment once her father had passed away. "He did not leave her any fortune? No wealth or situation to speak of?"

A darkness crossed Lady Havisham's face and Jonathan knew he already had his answer. Clearly his mother was displeased with the situation that her companion had found herself in. That was not surprising. Despite his frustrations with her, Jonathan knew that his mother had a gentle, compassionate heart.

"She never married? Or had opportunity?"

"Not as yet, no."

Jonathan hid a smile as the door opened to allow in the maid with the tea trays. His mother was always so very optimistic and even now was clearly hoping that her companion would find a suitable match and situation rather than remain in service. It would be one thing to hope for such a thing if the lady was of the right age, but to consider a lady who had already passed by her most eligible years was quite another!

"Ah, there you are!"

Lady Havisham's voice rang out as she sat up in her chair and beckoned someone forward. Jonathan turned his head just as a young lady stepped into the room.

His heart slammed hard against his chest. Who was this remarkable creature? She was dressed in a simple day dress although her gentle curves were more than apparent. Her very dark hair was pulled back from her face, highlighting the alabaster of her skin. Her brown eyes jumped from Lady Havisham to his own and then cast downward to the floor as she walked forward, her hands held gently in front of her.

This cannot be... Jonathan's eyes flared as he realized

that *this* was his mother's companion. He had assumed that she would be a good deal older, that she would have been closer to his own mother's age, but it appeared that he had been quite mistaken. His mind began to whirl with questions as regarded the lady. Why had she not already had her own Season? Why was she here with his mother rather than making her come out in London?

"Might I present Miss Deborah Fullerton?" When Jonathan caught his mother's eye, he saw her knowing smile and felt his stomach twist. "Miss Fullerton is my companion and has been so these last few years. I was once friends with her aunt, the late Miss Uddingston, and promised that should it be required, I would take on Miss Fullerton as my own companion. It *was* required and we have found ourselves both very happy, I think."

Miss Fullerton smiled but her cheeks flared with color as she caught Jonathan's eyes.

"I am very glad to meet you, my Lord." Bobbing a curtsey, she kept her head bowed low as he attempted to respond. His tongue felt too big for his mouth, shock still rippling through him and sending sparks to his fingers and toes. Clearing his throat gruffly, he got to his feet and bowed, although he did not hold out his hand toward her as he might have done with other guests.

"Miss Fullerton."

"Miss Fullerton, my son, the Earl of Havisham."

She curtsied again, then dropped her head as her cheeks burned with color, realizing her mistake.

"Thank you for permitting me to reside here for the Season, my Lord."

Jonathan opened his mouth to say that he had not had any knowledge of their arrival but then quickly shut it again, deciding that it would be unwise to say anything given her clear embarrassment.

"But of course, my dear," his mother said, firmly. "Now, sit to take tea with us. You will be very weary from the journey I expect, since I too feel rather fatigued."

Jonathan jumped up. There was no longer a desire to stay with his mother and take tea with her no, not when so much shock was still running through him.

"I will dine with you later, mother." Seeing the flickering frown on his mother's face, he bent over her hand. "I have much business to see to and if I am to dine with you this evening, then I must complete it this afternoon so that I have nothing but my freedom this evening."

Lady Havisham sighed but nodded.

"Very well. I shall stay here with Miss Fullerton. Until this evening, then?"

Nodding, Jonathan dared not cast another glance towards Miss Fullerton for fear that he would say something foolish and embarrass himself. The surprise that had overcome him upon seeing her had still not dissipated and as he walked to the door, Jonathan found his hands clenching and unclenching in a vain attempt to rid himself of all that he felt.

"She is not reaching her dotage, then." Closing the door behind him, Jonathan continued to mutter to himself as he walked back towards his study. "Why ever would such a lady become a companion rather than join society as she ought?"

A line formed between his brows as he struggled to push away the many questions which now burned in his mind. He had no need to have them answered. The lady was his mother's companion, nothing more. Why she was a companion and not out in society was not his business. The only thing that was required of him was to make certain that she was cared for by his staff and given all that was needed so that she, in turn, could take care of his mother.

Jonathan passed one hand over his eyes. Miss Fullerton was a rather pretty young lady and that had not escaped his notice. He was not a man inclined towards dalliances and certainly, he would not do so with any young lady who had been forced into becoming a companion rather than take their place in society as they ought. All the same, Jonathan was quite certain that the young lady would become something of a distraction for him, should he permit it. Letting out another groan of frustration, Jonathan gave himself a shake and then walked directly back to his study.

This Season was going to be difficult enough with his mother present, but now, with Miss Fullerton residing with him, Jonathan was quite sure that it would be all the more trying. Slamming his study door shut, Jonathan stalked towards his desk and sat down before reaching for his decanter and pouring himself a brandy.

This was going to be a very complicated Season indeed.

CHAPTER TWO

*D*eborah pinched her cheeks and then immediately dropped her hands, grimacing. It was no good. Regardless of what she tried, she still looked very pale indeed and, no doubt, Lady Havisham would remark upon it, just as she had done every previous morning since they had arrived.

Sighing, she folded her hands in her lap and considered her reflection. She was still rather tired from the long carriage journey to London but, in addition, there had been a great deal to do in the days following. They had now been in London for a sennight and had been out in town every single day. There had been various shops to visit, walks to take, and carriage rides to enjoy, although Lady Havisham seemed to spend most of her time peering out of the window and banging on the roof of the carriage in an attempt to get the driver to slow down even more.

There had been very little time spent in Lord Havisham's company.

Do you think him handsome?

Deborah tilted her head, considering the question she

had asked herself. She had been all too aware of his presence when they had first met, for Lord Havisham was quite a bit taller than herself, with broad shoulders and a solidness about his frame which made him something of a formidable presence. His eyes were a very vivid green, standing out starkly against the white gold of his hair. There was certainly a similarity in his coloring with that of his mother, but Deborah supposed that the square jaw and broad, slightly crooked nose came from his father. If she were to speak honestly, then Deborah would have to admit that there was an attractiveness in Lord Havisham's features and his dress.

The gentleman was always very well dressed and was certainly very fashionable in terms of the cut of his clothing, but there was an air of smugness about him which Deborah disliked. Whenever he came into a room and saw that she or his mother were present, he would lift his head a little higher and drop his shoulders a little lower as though to look down upon her as he walked past. He had never enquired after her health, showed no interest in her presence, and spoke to his mother only of his own interactions or present interests. It was as though she were quite invisible to him and that irritated Deborah terribly. Yes, she was a companion, but that did not mean that she was not to be acknowledged! Even an occasional 'good morning' would suffice. Her lip curled slightly.

Handsome but arrogant. She shook her head. *Which does not make him particularly likable.*

Sighing, Deborah rose to her feet and tried to push away her thoughts. Lady Havisham had not mentioned the subject to Deborah as yet, but she was all too aware that the lady still had every intention of having her make a match with Lord Havisham – and to Deborah's mind, the idea itself was quite preposterous.

"Enough, now."

Making her way to the door, Deborah drew in a long breath, set her shoulders, pasted a smile onto her face, and walked out of her bedchamber. Her slippered feet were quiet as she made her way to the staircase, her hand gliding down the rail. Lady Havisham would be in the dining room, Deborah expected, and they would break their fast together as they had done all of the previous mornings. Deborah liked to be there a few minutes before Lady Havisham, as a good companion ought, and so she quickened her steps, making her way past Lord Havisham's study.

The door opened unexpectedly, and Lord Havisham strode out, his head bent forward, muttering aloud – and walked straight into Deborah.

Something cold splashed over her gown and Deborah fell back with the force of walking straight into such a solid and tall person. A yelp of surprise escaped her as she stumbled against the wall.

"Good gracious!" Lord Havisham jumped forward – but it was not to catch Deborah. Putting out one hand towards a large, beautifully decorated china vase which was sitting atop a small, wooden table, he waited until he could be certain that it was neither going to wobble or fall, leaving Deborah to try to gather herself and recover from the shock of what had taken place. Her eyes strayed to the empty glass that Lord Havisham held in his other hand. Whatever had been in there was now soaking through her gown. That, as well as her cold skin, sent a shiver all through her. "Whatever were you doing, Miss Fullerton?"

Lord Havisham's voice was hard, his eyes a little narrowed as he gestured towards the china vase.

"You could have knocked this over completely! It would have hit the floor and broken into a dozen pieces!"

Deborah blinked rapidly. The heat of anger was beginning to warm her skin already, her stomach twisting this way and that at the lack of consideration in his response to her.

"I do believe, my Lord, that you were not looking ahead of you," she responded through gritted teeth, forcing herself to speak quietly and without any hint of the rising anger that she felt. "You were unaware of my presence, I think."

Lord Havisham's frown darkened, his jaw tightening for a few seconds before he responded.

"Miss Fullerton, you may have been used to wandering through my mother's estate without a care, but in this house, you ought to be a good deal more aware!" His eyes traveled to the large damp stain on the waist of her gown and the heat of her anger swiftly turned to embarrassment. "Perhaps then you would not be required to return to your bedchamber to change and be late to join my mother!"

With that exclamation, Lord Havisham moved quickly away, walking past her without so much as a glance or a murmur of concern for her situation. Deborah's hands tightened but she closed her eyes and kept her mouth closed for fear that, in her anger, she would say something inappropriate to Lord Havisham.

How dare he blame me?

She would have to change her gown, but Deborah had no intention of being tardy for Lady Havisham. Walking forward, she continued to the dining room and, upon entering, was relieved to see that she was the only one present.

"I shall beg to be excused for a few minutes once Lady Havisham has arrived," she murmured, glancing at the large mirror on the wall and finding the heat of embarrassment again beginning to bite at her cheeks.

"Good gracious, Miss Fullerton!" Deborah turned just as Lady Havisham came into the room. "Whatever has happened, my dear?"

Deborah opened her mouth to state the truth, such as she had seen it, but then quickly closed it again. It would not be wise to speak poorly of Lord Havisham to his mother.

"An accident only." She smiled ruefully, then spread her hands. "I must beg to excuse myself."

"But why did you not go at once?" Lady Havisham shooed her towards the door. "You will be cold!"

"I did not want to be tardy." Deborah's shoulders slumped as she realized just how much Lord Havisham's words had troubled her heart. "I was afraid you would be waiting and given that I am meant to join you for breakfast on time, I thought it would be a little poor of me to be so very late."

Lady Havisham's eyes widened and, reaching out, she caught one of Deborah's hands.

"My dear girl, you must not think of yourself in such terms! There is no *requirement* for you to join me here, although I do hope that you will continue to do so since I very much enjoy your company! I will never reprimand you for being late or for choosing not to appear at all, should you wish for a morning's rest." Her eyes were now filled with concern and as she pressed Deborah's hand, something shifted in her expression. "I do hope that my son has not been saying anything that might make you so concerned?" Deborah pressed her lips tight together as she fought to find something to say which would neither be the full truth nor a complete lie. "And was *this* my son's doing also?" Lady Havisham's voice was a little higher pitched now as she gestured to Deborah's gown. "You must tell me the truth, Miss Fullerton."

"It was an accident only." She tried to smile but felt it falter. "Lord Havisham was very busy and did not see that I was walking towards him. The glass he held in his hand was subsequently upturned and...." With a drop of her head, she gestured to her gown. "I should go to change."

Lady Havisham did not release her hand.

"And somehow, in the conversation which followed thereafter, he managed to make you feel as though you ought to make your way here first, rather than go to change?" Deborah could not do anything other than nod, dropping her head a little lower in embarrassment. In trying to do what was right, she had managed to upset Lady Havisham and would, no doubt, now find that her acknowledgment of this would lead to further difficulty. "Hmm." Lady Havisham's brows flickered low over her eyes. "Go and change, Miss Fullerton, but do not make too much haste. There is something I wish to discuss with my son, and it would be best if you were not present."

"Please." Deborah stepped forward. "I do not want to cause any difficulty between you and Lord Havisham. It is only a little matter and I –"

"My son will not be permitted to make you feel belittled and concerned over being tardy, Miss Fullerton." Lady Havisham's eyes glinted with anger. "You have been an excellent companion to me and, as you know, I have every intention of making a match with you and my son – although if he continues on in such a way, I fear that it will never come to pass."

Wondering if she should speak openly, Deborah pressed Lady Havisham's hand.

"Lady Havisham, that is indeed a very kind thought,

and you cannot know the full extent of my gratitude that you would even *think* of such a thing for someone such as I but, equally, there is no eagerness on my part to be connected to your son." She licked her lips, seeing Lady Havisham's frown and fearful now that she had offended the lady. "That is not to say that I believe it to be at all your doing in any way but –"

"You think him selfish."

Deborah nodded.

"I have always done so. Ever since I have been your companion, I have seen how eagerly you have waited for his arrival, for a letter to inform you of his whereabouts and his undertakings – but you received none. It has been near three years since you have been in each other's company for it was just before I became your companion, was it not?" A little less concerned, Deborah continued with more confidence. "And even now, the only reason that you find yourself in your son's company was simply because he did not know of your arrival, having misplaced the letter that you sent. Had he received it, do you believe that he would still have been here in London?"

Lady Havisham closed her eyes.

"You are not mistaken in your assertion, Miss Fullerton." Her shoulders dropped. "It is not a mistake to believe my son selfish."

"And on top of which, I am, at present, entirely ignored by him." Throwing up her hands, Deborah allowed her exasperation free. "I am all too aware of my social standing, Lady Havisham, but have found such a generous and kind spirit in you, and such a contentedness with your household, that I cannot help but express my gratitude. However, Lord Havisham does not so much as greet me! It is as though I am below the status of a servant, for at least they are acknowledged! But I remain as if I am a shadow and nothing more. This incident," she gestured to her gown, "was entirely his fault for he walked directly from his study without so much as lifting his head to look ahead of him and yet, somehow, he concocted something quite ridiculous as to why the fault was mine." Shaking her head, Deborah closed her eyes. "Forgive me, Lady Havisham, for speaking too bluntly but I fear I must tell you the truth." Opening her eyes, she looked directly back at Lady Havisham and took in a deep breath. "I find Lord Havisham arrogant, selfish, prideful, and with a disdain for others which I cannot overlook. In short, Lady Havisham, I do not think I could ever marry such a gentleman."

Lady Havisham sighed.

"Then you wish me to drop the scheme?"

Deborah swallowed hard. To state that yes, she wished her to do so might very well leave her in her present situation for the rest of her days – but the truth was, even if she were offered Lord Havisham's hand, Deborah did not think she could accept. That would bring her a life of misery and, even though her situation was not as she had once hoped, it would be better than tying herself to such a gentleman for the rest of her life!

"I do, Lady Havisham."

The lady closed her eyes but nodded.

"I cannot blame you for such a decision, Miss Fullerton. There is not one word of a lie in anything that you have said."

"I did not mean to injure you in saying such things. I hope I have not done."

Lady Havisham laughed but it was a sad, broken sound.

"You have not. You have only told me of the very same observations that are within my own mind. However, that does not mean that I will give up my plan for you entirely, Miss Fullerton!" Sounding a good deal brighter, Lady Havisham smiled back at her. "If you are not to wed my son, then I shall have to find someone much more improved than he to match you with."

Swamped with relief that she was not to lose her opportunity entirely, Deborah looked down, squeezed her eyes closed and tried to laugh.

"Thank you, Lady Havisham. That is very kind of you."

"You did not think that I would turn away from such an endeavor just because you have rejected my son?" Lady Havisham's voice was soft, and Deborah lifted her head meekly, not wanting the lady to see the truth in her eyes. "Miss Fullerton, recall that I know all too well what your situation is. With your father as cruel and as harsh as he is, there is no circumstance on earth that would have me pushing you back towards him. What I have promised to you remains. Your father will know naught of my plan as we have agreed but I am determined that you shall find a happy and secure future, far from your present situation. I can well understand what you must be feeling at present, given that I too was once a companion."

Deborah nodded.

"I remember."

"I was fortunate enough to find an excellent husband and I am determined that you shall be given the same chance. You are much too young and beautiful to remain a companion, Miss Fullerton. Have no fear. We will succeed, albeit without you joining *my* family which was my dearest wish."

Taking in a deep breath, Deborah let it out slowly, blinking back the hot tears which had formed in her eyes.

"Thank you, Lady Havisham."

The lady reached out and patted her hand.

"But of course. Now go and change your gown before you catch a cold! And do not rush back, there is no need for haste."

A sharp glint came into her eye and Deborah laughed, relieved now that she had been able to speak of Lord Havisham without having to hold back from the truth.

"I shall make sure I am entirely presentable, Lady Havisham," she promised, as the lady let go of her hand. "Do excuse me."

Deborah walked out of Lady Havisham's presence and made her way back to her bedchamber. But this time, there was a smile on her face and a joyous relief in her heart that Lady Havisham had understood her reluctance towards Lord Havisham, and had not tried to force the match. There was still hope for her yet, and that was a great relief to Deborah indeed.

CHAPTER THREE

That was my fault entirely.

Jonathan grimaced as he glanced down at the empty glass in his hand. He ought not to have blamed the lady, but he had been so mortified at his own foolishness that he had found himself saying such things to her without being able to stop himself. His hand was damp, and he gave it a small shake, striding towards the library without hesitation.

Swinging the door open, he stepped inside and allowed himself a moment or two to breathe in the stillness. In the first week of his mother and Miss Fullerton being present in his home, Jonathan had struggled not to notice the young lady. She was always very quiet indeed, but that did not mean that he was easily able to ignore her. Why had his mother not hired an older lady for a companion? Why must she have taken on such a young lady? It was rather unfair on the latter, Jonathan considered, for she would have to be in amongst society where the gentlemen would observe her and see her gentle looks but then be informed that she was a companion and, thus, would forget her entirely.

Jonathan frowned. He did not know much about the young lady's background, save for the fact that she was the daughter of a Viscount. That was all his mother had told him, and yet there must be some reason for her to be a paid companion rather than out in society in her own right. Jonathan had never considered asking his mother anything more about Miss Fullerton's situation, but mayhap he ought to do so.

Although it is not as though I have shown any interest in her up until this moment.

His lips twisted. Miss Fullerton was not his companion and thus, Jonathan had chosen to make very little of her presence. If his mother wished to have a companion, then the lady was *her* responsibility and had nothing whatsoever to do with Jonathan himself. Running his fingers over the books on one of the many, many shelves, Jonathan tried to turn his thoughts from Miss Fullerton and think about his reasons for coming to the library in the first place, but the guilt rushing through his heart simply would not leave him. He should not have blamed the lady, should not have said such things about her being tardy for his mother. That had been uncalled for, and he had seen the flash of hurt in her eyes.

I ought to apologize.

The very idea hit hard against him, and Jonathan had to fight through it, telling himself that even though he did not wish to, it would be the right thing to do. If he did not, then the guilt would linger within him and he would struggle to fight against it, every time he saw her. No, it would be wise for him simply to make amends and, thereafter, continue with his own endeavors.

"Only a word or two will suffice," he told himself,

turning back towards the door. "She does not need more than that."

The only reason he was doing so was for his own sake rather than for hers and, striding from the room, Jonathan made his way purposefully towards the dining room.

The sound of his mother's voice stopped him.

"It is not a mistake to believe my son selfish."

He stopped, his hand reaching out for the door handle but finding himself suddenly unwilling to step inside. His heart twisted but Jonathan attempted to ignore the dull ache that came thereafter. There was some truth in that statement, and it was not one that he wished to ignore. In behaving as he did and in making certain that he was not often in his mother's company, Jonathan could well understand why she thought him selfish. After all, all such choices had been done simply for his own benefit, so that *he* would not have to endure any fragment of difficulty or annoyance.

His mouth bunched to one side.

Then why does it irritate me to hear it?

"And on top of which, I am, at present, entirely ignored by him. I am all too aware of my social standing, Lady Havisham, but have found such a generous and kind spirit in you, and such a contentedness with your household, that I cannot help but express my gratitude. However, Lord Havisham does not so much as greet me!"

Jonathan's lips flattened, his hand falling to his side as he heard Miss Fullerton speak. It was not her place to speak so, and he fully expected his mother to reprimand her for doing so – but Miss Fullerton continued, unhindered.

"It is as though I am below the status of a servant, for at least they are acknowledged! But I remain as if I am a shadow and nothing more. This incident was entirely his fault, for he walked directly from his study without so much as lifting his head to look ahead of him and yet, somehow, he concocted something quite ridiculous as to why the fault was mine." A piercing heat rammed itself through Jonathan's chest and he took a small step back from the door, as if she had reached out and struck him. How dare she speak to his mother in such a way? Whether or not it was the truth, Miss Fullerton ought to have more respect for his position as well as being aware of her own. "Forgive me, Lady Havisham, for speaking too bluntly, but I fear I must tell you the truth. I find Lord Havisham arrogant, selfish, prideful, and with a disdain for others that I cannot overlook. In short, Lady Havisham, I do not think I could ever marry such a gentleman."

The tightness in Jonathan's chest grew. Marry? Why should he ever think of marrying a companion – and why indeed should Miss Fullerton even consider such a thing given her position in his household? He wanted to laugh, to shake his head in mirth, but his lips refused to pull themselves upwards. Instead, the harsh words she had spoken seemed to fling themselves at him repeatedly, leaving him bruised. Dropping his head, Jonathan ran one hand through his hair and then turned on his heel to walk away.

"Then you wish me to drop the scheme?"

The final few words floated towards him, and Jonathan let out a small groan which he muffled quickly with his hand for fear of being overheard. His mother was a part of this plan, then. *That* was why Miss Fullerton had mentioned matrimony. Lady Havisham had thought to bring about a betrothal, clearly considering Miss Fullerton to be the right sort of young lady for him. Last Season, she had come to London and then to Bath in an attempt to introduce him to Miss Fullerton, although Jonathan had done all he could to avoid her and had thus brought an end to such a plan for *that* year, at least. Again, Jonathan tried to laugh, but the sound would not come. Instead, he was angry, irritated, and upset. Whether or not Miss Fullerton thought well of him, she had no right to inform his mother of her opinion of his character! And his mother had no right to encourage Miss Fullerton to consider him as a potential suitor!

Arrogant, selfish, prideful, and with a disdain for others which I cannot overlook.

His mouth tugged to one side as he rushed back into the library, slamming the door hard behind him. Storming across the room, he attempted to sit down in a chair close to the cold hearth, but in the very next instant, he was standing and walking about the room again, in a temper.

"She is a companion," he said aloud, as though such a thing would help him to consider the truth in its fullness. "It matters not what she thinks of you." Lifting his chin, he began to pace up and down the library floor, albeit with slow, heavy steps. "Even if your own mother agrees with her, what does it matter? Why are you allowing her words to injure you so?"

His spoken words did not bring him any answers. As much as Jonathan wanted to remove such thoughts from his mind and return to his own considerations, he simply could not. Those words from Miss Fullerton had struck down hard into his heart and refused to be dislodged.

"My Lord?"

Jonathan swung around.

"You should knock, Armstrong," he muttered, waving a hand towards the butler.

"I did, my Lord." The butler cleared his throat in an uncharacteristic manner, catching Jonathan's attention all the more. "You have a visitor, and I did not want to leave him waiting for too long before I came to speak to you, my Lord."

Rifling another hand through his hair, Jonathan dropped it and then sighed.

"And who has come to call?"

"Lord Harrogate, my Lord."

Relieved that his friend had come at the precise time that Jonathan required distraction, he nodded.

"But of course. Show him in at once and send for a refreshments tray. He may well not yet have broken his fast."

Within a few minutes, Lord Harrogate walked into the library, a broad smile settling upon his face.

"Well, old boy! Today is the day, is it not?"

Jonathan frowned.

"What do you mean?"

Lord Harrogate's smile slipped, his eyes rounding a little.

"The day when the newly introduced young ladies of the *ton* come out! Pray do not tell me that you have forgotten!"

"Of course, I had not forgotten. It was only gone from my mind for a moment. I have been caught up with..." he waved a hand, "...another matter."

"But no matter can be as important as this!" Lord Harrogate exclaimed, making Jonathan chuckle, his troubles momentarily forgotten. "Come now, we are meant to be going into town, for I plan to purchase a new cravat for the occasion, and you assured me that you would do the same."

"I had *quite* forgotten that, I confess, but I will make ready just the same," Jonathan told him. "But come, let us eat a little together first, for I have not yet done so this morning."

Lord Harrogate hesitated, then sank down into a chair, choosing to let himself relax for a short while rather than hurry on back to the carriage.

"Very well. Mayhap you would like to share with me this other matter which has concerned you so?"

Jonathan shook his head.

"It is of no importance."

"It must be of *some* importance, if you have forgotten about the ball this evening because of it!"

He spread his hands, attempting to push away Lord Harrogate's questions.

"Pray, do not concern yourself." Seeing the gleam of interest in his friend's eye, Jonathan sighed inwardly and then tried to smile. "I have heard that a... young lady thinks rather poorly of my character, that is all."

Lord Harrogate's eyes flared in surprise.

"Indeed? But we have not long been in London and the Season has not yet properly begun! From where did you hear this? And from which young lady?"

Jonathan shook his head, waving his hands.

"No, no, I shall not give you the particulars! At present, I am attempting to push such thoughts from my mind and will not allow them to injure me further."

"I think it a most unladylike practice, to inform you of such a thing," Lord Harrogate retorted, sniffing as though the lady herself was present. "You will need to make certain that you stay far from this particular lady for she might then go on to say such things to one of her friends and then what would become of you? Rumors would spread and –"

"I do not think there is any need to concern myself in that regard, for the lady is quite discreet and only said so to a most trustworthy acquaintance. I overheard by mistake, that is all."

Tutting, Lord Harrogate pinned Jonathan with a sharp gaze. "You must not allow such words to frustrate you. They are all quite untrue, I am sure. Set the lady aside and go on to another." His lips quirked. "After all, I am certain that she meant very little to you. Perhaps only a fleeting interest?"

Something twisted in Jonathan's heart. "What do you mean?"

Lord Harrogate laughed and shrugged one shoulder, just as the maid brought in the tray of refreshments, setting it down before them.

"You have never cared one whit about any particular lady!" he exclaimed, still chuckling. "I would be *most* surprised if you should begin to consider one of them now. That would be rather concerning, I should think. I might have to summon the doctor to make sure that you were quite well."

This seemed to bring him a good deal of mirth and he laughed somewhat uproariously for a few minutes, whilst Jonathan could only summon the smallest of smiles. Lord Harrogate's words were quite true but after what he had overheard from Miss Fullerton, they seemed to sting a little more than he had expected.

"And pray tell, will this particular lady be at the ball this evening?" Lord Harrogate asked, one eyebrow lifting. "I do hope you will not be so melancholy then also!"

Jonathan's smile was fixed. "I am not certain, but I believe she may well be present," he replied, having not shown any interest in his mother's plans for the evening. "But it will not be difficult to avoid her. It is not as though society thinks particularly highly of her."

Lord Harrogate's smile faded and the triumph that had briefly flashed through Jonathan's heart at such a spiteful remark drained away, leaving him feeling small even in his friend's eyes. Again, he questioned silently why Miss Fullerton's words had struck him so, but still, the answer would not come. It was most frustrating, and Jonathan could only hope that, with an evening of dancing and entertainment waiting for him, he would soon be able to forget about the lady entirely.

CHAPTER FOUR

"Good evening, my Lord."

Deborah did not even try to smile as Lord Havisham walked into the drawing-room. In fact, she averted her eyes entirely and did not see the startled look which spread across his face, and was then swiftly followed by a flood of color to his cheeks.

She was less inclined to be in Lord Havisham's company than ever before, now that she had spoken honestly to his mother about her opinion of him and found naught but understanding there. On top of which, this evening was to be the first ball she attended with Lady Havisham, and Deborah was already looking forward to being in amongst society. Now that she knew Lady Havisham was hopeful of securing another match for her, in the place of Lord Havisham, there was a little more excitement within her heart.

It is just as well that father does not know of my whereabouts.

Sighing inwardly, she turned away from Lord Havisham entirely, having no expectation of his responding to her. Her life as a companion had been a blessed one, thanks solely to the kindness of Lady Havisham's heart and her eagerness to take Deborah on as her companion. Her father, determined that he should make some money from his daughter, was given a small sum each month, but Lady Havisham pressed a good deal more into Deborah's hand. It kept her father at bay, and Deborah was more than grateful for Lady Havisham's kindness.

"You are attending the ball this evening, then?"

Deborah glanced back at Lord Havisham, a little surprised at his conversation.

"Yes, I am."

"*With* my mother?"

She blinked.

"Yes."

"Even though I am to be in attendance?"

Heat tore through Deborah's chest, spiraling up into her neck.

"That is so, Lord Havisham."

She did not give any further explanation but neither did she turn her back to him again, lifting her chin just a little as she looked steadily into his eyes. Lord Havisham grimaced and then turned away, leaving Deborah to close her eyes in frustration, forcing back the sharp questions which sprang to her lips. Did he not wish her to attend? Or was he thinking that, once more, she did not know her place?

"Ah, there we are!" Lady Havisham sailed into the room, her eyes bright with excitement. "And Miss Fullerton, you look quite lovely."

Deborah smoothed her gown, aware that this was yet again, another evidence of Lady Havisham's kindness. She had insisted that she buy a few new gowns for Deborah and, upon doing so, had instructed Deborah to don the very best one for this evening. Deborah had done so with delight and was now clad in a gentle lilac dress with hints of grey running through it. There was even a little lace at the neckline, making her feel as if she were worthy of stepping out into society.

"Miss Fullerton tells me that she is to accompany you this evening, mother."

Lord Havisham's voice lifted in a question even though he did not speak one. Lady Havisham's smile flickered.

"Yes, of course she is to attend."

"But there is no need," Lord Havisham continued, gesturing towards Deborah as if she were not able to hear him. "*I* am going to be in attendance."

Lady Havisham's lip curled gently.

"And you intend to make certain that I am never without good company, is that so?"

"No, it is only to say that you would have good company regardless of whether or not Miss Fullerton attends," came the reply, as Deborah dropped her head and looked down at the floor, her hands clasping tightly together. "Your *companion* does not need to join us."

The way that he emphasized that particular word had heat searing Deborah's cheeks with such force that she caught her breath, hating the fact that tears were burning behind her eyes. Blinking rapidly, she saw her evening curl up into a ball and then shatter before her. She would have to remain here, and the ball would go on without her. If Lord Havisham did not wish her to attend, then she could not go against his wishes.

"Deborah." Her throat tight, she forced herself to look up to where Lady Havisham was standing. The lady did not often use her forename, but the significance of it was not lost on her. Lady Havisham's cheeks held two red spots and her eyes were blazing. "Deborah, I wish you to ignore everything my son has said and make your way to the carriage."

Swallowing, Deborah dared a glance towards Lord Havisham. He had closed his eyes and was in the process of letting out a long and frustrated breath – which Deborah presumed she was meant to hear.

"If you are quite certain," she began, but Lady Havisham astonished her still further by stamping her foot and jabbing one finger into Lord Havisham's chest.

"How dare you speak in such a way in front of Miss Fullerton? Have you no consideration at all?"

Deborah began to walk quickly past them, not wishing to embarrass either herself or Lord Havisham, even though he had been so cruel as to speak of her in such a way.

"Miss Fullerton has been with me when *you* were not. She has done a great deal for me, provided me with more companionship and friendship than I have enjoyed in years. In the absence of my son, I gained someone so very kind and sweet-natured that it took some of my pain and sorrow away." Deborah reached the door, but Lady Havisham held out one hand, palm outwards. "Wait a moment. I will make one thing clear to my son and in your presence also, Miss Fullerton."

Nodding, Deborah clasped her hands behind her, uncertain as to where to look. Lord Havisham was glaring fixedly at the wall just behind his mother's shoulder, whilst Lady Havisham had planted both hands on her hips, her chin jutting forward.

"Miss Fullerton may be my companion, but I have every intention of finding her a suitable match this Season." Deborah flushed hot, her eyes closing as she kept her head low. She could only pray that Lady Havisham would not think to mention that she had once thought her son to be the right husband for Deborah, else she might have to turn and flee, such would be her mortification. "I am certain that I have already spoken to you of Miss Fullerton's situation, but if you do not recall, permit me to remind you. Miss Fullerton is the daughter of Viscount Ingleby and thus has every right to be in amongst society, just as you do. She is attending this evening as an equal and you should treat her as such."

Lord Havisham sniffed.

"If that is so, then why does not Viscount Ingleby accompany his daughter into town?" His eyes darted towards Deborah, catching her gaze for a moment before spiraling away again. "Is it an issue of wealth?"

I do not think I could feel more ashamed.

Hearing Lady Havisham's swift intake of breath, Deborah waited for the response. She knew that Lady Havisham would never give away any confidences for, whilst she was fully aware of Deborah's situation, there had always been an unspoken promise that it would not be made well known.

"I believe that in the three years we have been apart from each other, you have become thoughtless." Lady Havisham's voice had softened but Deborah could hear the pain in her words. "I did not think that my son would ever speak with such bluntness in front of the lady herself." One hand gestured towards Deborah but she herself could not so much as look at Lord Havisham. "For what it is worth, Lord Ingleby has more than enough wealth to bring his daughter out into society." Deborah held her breath, her eyes squeezing closed as her heart began to hammer furiously. Silently, she pleaded with Lady Havisham not to say more. The lady did not fail her. "But not all gentlemen are kind-hearted, Havisham." Lady Havisham's words appeared now to be directed solely towards her son, as though she feared that the very gentleman she described was now standing before her. "Some are inconsiderate, bearing grudges, holding resentments, and punishing those who do not deserve it. They think only of themselves and of *their* standing, making certain that not even a single kindness is shown to anyone they deem unworthy. And that, my dear son, is why Miss Fullerton has been *forced* to become my companion. It is only by God's grace that I heard of her father's intentions for her and was able to make the arrangements to have her come and live with me."

Lord Havisham did not react other than to clear his throat and return his gaze to his mother. Deborah could only glance at him before dropping her eyes to the floor again.

"Then I take it her father –" Stopping abruptly, he coughed for a moment. "I mean to say, *your* father, Miss Fullerton, is unaware of my mother's intentions at present?"

No matter how much she tried, Deborah could not find the courage to look into his face. He had made her feel so very insignificant that she could only drag her gaze to his shoulder.

"My father believes me to be simply a companion to Lady Havisham."

"And therefore, he should not be informed of such intentions?"

"No!"

Deborah's exclamation was matched by that of Lady Havisham.

"No, he is not to know anything of it until it is much too late," Lady Havisham said firmly, as Deborah pressed both hands to her cheeks, feeling them hot and herself unsteady. "You must give me your word, Havisham."

"I do not understand –"

"I do not care whether or not you understand! You must give me your word."

Her heart was beating so furiously that Deborah was sure that the sound of it echoed around the room. Desperately, she found the strength to look into Lord Havisham's face and saw him looking back at her with a frown of confusion creasing his brow.

But then he nodded, and Deborah closed her eyes in relief.

"You have my word, of course." There was a gentleness in his voice that Deborah had not heard before, and her relief was so overwhelming that she thought she might sink to the floor. "Forgive me for my previous harshness, Miss Fullerton."

She could not speak. The audacity of his request, so simply given when he had been so blunt, so cruel in his words, meant that she was unable to answer him.

"We should depart." Lady Havisham's briskness broke the awkwardness and, the next moment, Deborah felt her arm being grasped gently as she fell into step with Lady Havisham. "The ball will not wait. I think, Havisham, that Miss Fullerton and I will take the carriage alone. We will send it back for you."

Deborah did not dare glance behind her, quite certain that Lord Havisham would explode with irritation at such a demand – but Lady Havisham's words were met with nothing but silence.

"Come, the carriage will be waiting." Lady Havisham's arm slipped around Deborah's shoulders, comforting and calming as though she were her daughter and Lady Havisham her mother. "And you shall have the most excellent evening, I am sure."

Deborah could only nod, her heart still pounding furiously and her head already beginning to ache. Lord Havisham had proven to her, once again, that he was not the sort of gentleman she could ever consider marrying. His harsh manner and lack of consideration was an indication of a character lacking any sort of kindness.

She only hoped that she could trust Lord Havisham's word, for if he betrayed it, then Deborah knew her future would be very dark indeed.

CHAPTER FIVE

"And who is the young lady that your mother is presenting to Lord Blake?"

Jonathan cleared his throat.

"That is Miss Deborah Fullerton, daughter of Viscount Ingleby."

"Might I ask who she is in relation to your mother?"

Glancing at his friend, Jonathan hesitated. This was now the third ball that they had attended together and still, he was unsure as to how to introduce the young lady.

"Miss Fullerton resides with my mother at present, assisting her in some matters."

A small frown flickered across Lord Thornley's face.

"Then she is a companion?"

Again, came the hesitation.

"If you are wondering whether or not she is out, then the answer to such a question is yes, she is." Jonathan saw the gleam in Lord Thornley's eyes, caught the way his lips curved into a half-smile. "I am certain that she would be very pleased to make your acquaintance."

"Thank you." Lord Thornley cleared his throat and pulled back his shoulders. "Do excuse me."

Jonathan nodded but said nothing, watching as Lord Thornley made his way directly towards Miss Fullerton. His mother greeted the gentleman eagerly, having already been introduced some time ago. Sighing inwardly, Jonathan turned his head away and walked across the room, thinking that he might go in search of a game of cards rather than linger in this room. Another sennight had passed, which now made it a fortnight since his mother had arrived in London. A fortnight of being in Miss Fullerton's company and a fortnight of finding his life a good deal more complicated than before.

"Good evening, Lord Havisham."

Stopping, Jonathan smiled at the young ladies who each studied him with a keen eye. He knew two of them, with the first being the daughter of Viscount Anglesey and the second the daughter of the Earl of Marlock.

"Good evening, Miss Docherty, Lady Vivian." Sweeping a bow, he glanced at the third. "Pray introduce me to your friend."

Lady Vivian, with her bright smile and vivid blue eyes was the first to oblige him.

"Might I present Miss Judith Newfield, daughter of Viscount Kintore."

Jonathan bowed towards the young lady who, he noted, did not smile at him as she rose from her curtsey.

"Good evening, Miss Newfield. I am glad to make your acquaintance."

"As am I," she murmured, although that expected smile still did not touch her lips.

"Miss Newfield lives in Scotland, and finds London to be very dreary indeed compared to the wind and the waves that crash along the cliffs near to her father's estate," Miss Docherty smiled, her eyes dancing as Jonathan grinned. "But we must try to improve things for her!"

Miss Newfield's lips turned upwards but only briefly.

"London suits me very well, I thank you."

"And is your father present in London with you?"

She flinched as though he had struck her.

"My father has lately taken ill," she answered, her eyes darting to his and then away again. "We are here in the hope that a London doctor will be able to improve his health." Her vague smile faded entirely. "He insisted that I come out this evening, even though I would much prefer to be by his side."

"You must not appear ungrateful, however," Miss Docherty said quickly but Jonathan only shook his head.

"Indeed, I quite understand, Miss Newfield." The way that she looked at him told him that she was not quite sure if his words could be trusted. "There is a duty required to one's parents that we feel very deeply, do we not?"

A duty that I have failed in entirely.

"And is that why your mother is present this Season?" Lady Vivian asked, taking Jonathan's attention away. "And does she have a young lady with her?"

"That is Miss Fullerton," Jonathan replied, wishing that the lady had not mentioned Miss Fullerton, so that he would not now have to make explanation. He had been attempting to push all thought of Miss Fullerton away, only now to have to now go into yet another explanation. "She has been... residing with my mother these past few years but is now come to London."

"Oh." Lady Vivian's nose crinkled gently as though she did not want to be in any way associated with someone that was so clearly a companion. "Then Miss Fullerton, I am sure, must be very busy indeed making certain that—" Her eyes widened. "Good gracious, is she going to dance?"

Jonathan's head swiveled around, catching sight of Lord Thornley leading Miss Fullerton out to the middle of the room where a few other couples were waiting, clearly ready and waiting to dance.

"It seems that they are, yes," he replied, a little astonished himself but refusing to allow such astonishment into his voice. "I am sure Miss Fullerton is an excellent dancer."

Lady Vivian's eyes widened still as she looked back at Jonathan.

"But you cannot be contented with a mere companion standing up in such a fashion!" she exclaimed, as Jonathan shook his head. "I am sure that you will be required to speak to the young lady at length later this evening."

Quite what this matter has to do with you, I am not sure.

Jonathan did not speak such a sentence out loud but instead merely shrugged.

"Miss Fullerton is the daughter of a Viscount and, as such, has every right to dance if she wishes," he stated, as Lady Vivian's eyes narrowed slightly. "She is the daughter of Viscount Ingleby and, therefore, quite eligible."

"I see." Lady Vivian searched his face as if she were trying to find out an answer that he was refusing to speak to her. "And you say that this lady resides with you at present?"

"With my mother," Jonathan clarified, wondering why this seemed to matter such a great deal. "I should now take my leave. I —"

"Might you wish to take a turn with me about the room, Lord Havisham?" Lady Vivian's eyes were now fixed to his, giving him very little option but to agree. "My mother is nearby, but she will not be displeased with such a thing, so long as we stay within this room," Lady Vivian continued, as Miss Docherty's cheeks flushed and Miss Newfield looked away, perhaps a little embarrassed by the lady's forwardness. "I am not inclined towards dancing this evening as yet, but mayhap a short turn would do me very well."

Jonathan blinked, then cleared his throat in an attempt to remove the surprise from both his expression and his voice.

"But of course."

With a small inclination of his head, he offered the lady his arm and she accepted it at once. A bright smile was quickly pinned to her lips as she fell into step beside him, although Jonathan did not have any of the same delight. He had been eager to go in search of cards rather than spend time in company – particularly in the company of a young lady whom he found rather forward in both manner and conversation.

"Tell me, Lord Havisham, do you intend to run away to Bath this Season?"

He glanced down at her in surprise.

"Bath?"

She nodded, her eyes darting up to his as a coy smile tugged lightly at one corner of her lips.

"I have not forgotten, you know. I remember that you went to Bath last Season and left behind a good deal of upset!"

Grimacing, Jonathan tried to shrug off the matter.

"Indeed. I do recall, Lady Vivian, but it could not be helped."

Another glance up to his face, questions darting about in her eyes.

"You had no other choice but to go to Bath?"

"My mother wished to have the townhouse." It was a poor explanation but given that he felt very much obliged to give one to her, it was the only one he could come up with. "I thought to allow her a little time here in London without me."

"Although I believe she soon made her way to Bath, which was around the time you then returned to London – although it neared the end of the Season by that time which meant that there was very little opportunity to be in your company." Lady Vivian sounded aggrieved, as though she had taken the matter personally. "I do hope you will not do so again."

"I shall not be making my way to Bath, Lady Vivian," Jonathan told her, seeing the warm, delighted smile spread across her face as if his words had been a gift solely for her. "I fully intend to stay here in London."

Lady Vivian's hand tightened on his arm.

"You will be very welcome in my company whenever you can oblige me, Lord Havisham."

The warmth in her tone had his heart sending him a warning.

"You are very kind, Lady Vivian."

He did not say anything more, did not tell her anything that would be of any encouragement, but instead merely continued to walk with her, wondering silently when he might escape to the card room. His gaze suddenly snagged on the figure of Miss Fullerton, seeing her laughing up into Lord Thornley's face as they walked together across the room. She did not even glance in Jonathan's direction, did not appear to know that he was present, and yet Jonathan could not seem to pull his eyes away. Miss Fullerton was clad in a very pale green gown which Jonathan thought suited her well, for it drew a contrast between itself and her dark brown eyes, making them all the more appealing. The way that she was smiling at Lord Thornley made his gut twist, for she had never once smiled at him in such a way. It transformed her features, bringing light and warmth into her eyes and adding color to her cheeks. Jonathan did not like the twist of envy which ran through him upon seeing it and tried, therefore, to return his attention to Lady Vivian.

"I am sure that Lord Ingleby did not have a daughter."

A frown pulled at Jonathan's brow.

"I beg your pardon?"

"That is Miss Fullerton, is it not?" Lady Vivian lifted her chin in the direction of Miss Fullerton and Lord Thornley, perhaps having seen his attention caught in the very same direction. "She has been dancing with Lord Thornley and now seems to be very pleased indeed to have more of his company."

"I am sure she makes excellent conversation."

Lady Vivian's lip curled.

"As I have said, I do not recall that Lord Ingleby had a daughter."

Lifting one shoulder, Jonathan tried to brush aside the remark.

"I do not know the gentleman. My mother's affairs are her own."

"My father is acquainted with Lord Ingleby, and I am well aware that he only had two sons, just as a gentleman ought." Lady Vivian gave a small sniff, then glanced up at him, her eyes rounded with concern. "I can only hope that this particular young lady is not spreading untruths about her position in the hope of garnering *more* from your mother than she ought."

Jonathan shook his head.

"I am certain that my mother has done all that is

required of her to make certain that Miss Fullerton is quite suitable," he told her, more than confident in such a remark. "Although I thank you for your concern."

"It is strange, is it not, that Viscount Ingleby has never made mention of a daughter?" Lady Vivian moved a fraction closer to Jonathan so that he could feel the warmth of her spreading gently across his skin. "My father is connected with him, as you might be aware, but I am certain that in all of his dealings, a daughter has not been made mention of in any regard."

Not being able to answer this, Jonathan ran one hand over his forehead.

"There will be some reason for it." Recalling just how much his mother had said about Lord Ingleby, Jonathan tried to dismiss Lady Vivian's concerns. "We need not concern ourselves."

"Just so long as she is not some distant cousin of Lord Ingleby's who has lied about her need for a position in order to gain the favor of your mother."

A small needle of doubt stabbed itself into Jonathan's mind.

"I am sure that –"

"Both you and your dear mother have the very kindest of hearts, I am sure," Lady Vivian continued. "But mayhap you are unaware of Lord Ingleby's family, nor the fact that he has never mentioned a daughter to any of his acquaintances." Her hand squeezed his arm gently. "That is strange, is it not?"

Jonathan hesitated but then could not help but agree.

"It is. I am grateful for your concern, Lady Vivian, although I am quite certain there is nothing you need worry about. My mother is the most obliging creature, certainly, but she is diligent."

Despite his own words to Lady Vivian, Jonathan was unable to remove the doubt from his own mind. Why did Viscount Ingleby never mention a daughter? If that was true, then there must be a reason behind it. Was there any chance that Lord Ingleby did not have a daughter, as Lady Vivian had suggested, and that, therefore, Miss Fullerton was simply trading on his name in order to gain herself a better position?

"Thank you for walking with me, Lord Havisham."

Without realizing it, Jonathan had managed to accompany Lady Vivian back to her mother, suddenly aware of the other two young ladies now watching him with small, glimmering smiles. Frustrated that his thoughts had, once again, been caught up with Miss Fullerton, Jonathan gave Lady Vivian a warm smile, turning to bow over her hand.

"I should be glad of your company any time you wish to bestow it on me," he found himself saying, regretting the words the very moment they were spoken. "I do hope you enjoy the rest of the evening, Lady Vivian." Bowing, he released her hand and stepped away, heat rising in his face. He had not meant to give such a compliment to the lady and had only said as much to cover his own frustration at his considering of Miss Fullerton, yet again. The dazzling smile that Lady Vivian now offered him was confirmation of the fact that she had taken his remarks to heart and would now, no doubt, seek him out without any hesitation the next time they were in company together. Unable to find anything else to say, he bowed again – for what was now the second time – and then stepped away, his mortification complete.

"Lady Vivian is a lovely young lady, I must say."

Jonathan rolled his eyes as Lord Harrogate came to fall into step beside him.

"Lady Vivian asked me to walk with her around the

room," he stated, as Lord Harrogate's brows rose in surprise. "It was not my own choice, but I certainly could not refuse her either!"

"I suppose you could not." Lord Harrogate nodded to his left. "I see that Lord Thornley appears to be greatly interested in Miss Fullerton. I do not believe that he has left her side ever since his introduction!"

Jonathan grimaced.

"Indeed."

"I thought her only your mother's companion, but I hear she is the daughter of a Viscount and could very well be out this Season!"

"That is so."

"Then I think I ought to make myself known to her, given that she is so very lovely."

Jonathan's gut twisted.

"It is very kind of you to consider Miss Fullerton, I am sure, but she does not have any dowry to speak of. That must surely be a little disappointing."

Lord Harrogate laughed and slapped Jonathan good-naturedly on the back.

"As if I should care about such a thing! You know very well that I have adequate wealth and, whilst a dowry would be beneficial, it is not necessary."

Growing all the more frustrated, Jonathan shook his head firmly.

"You do not even wish to marry."

"Ah, but that is not quite the truth of it!" Lord Harrogate exclaimed. "Yes, it is quite truthful that I do not wish to wed any lady of quality, but when I see Miss Fullerton, my mind begins to wonder what it would be like to wed such a lady as she."

Jonathan turned and looked at his friend steadily. There

was something in Lord Harrogate's voice that he did not like although he could not quite place what it was.

"What do you mean?"

"Well...." Lord Harrogate tipped his head, his eyes darting away. "I have oft considered the fact that I must produce the heir and find the thought of a wife to be something of a bind. However," his eyes darted towards Miss Fullerton. "Given that she has been acting as a companion to your mother, I think that she must be rather biddable, quiet, and subservient. And what more could I want from a wife?"

Jonathan's stomach turned over, his jaw tightening.

"You think that if you take her as a wife, you can simply continue living as you please, without concern."

"Precisely! She will do as I ask without question, most likely be pleased to stay at the estate whilst I return very often to town, and will bear the required children for me and thus preserve the family line." The rage which began to boil up within Jonathan's heart was difficult to control. He could not explain it but the mere thought of Miss Fullerton being treated so brought such a fierce anger that it shot fire through each of his limbs, with his hands curling tightly into fists. "I shall make certain to speak to her at length this evening, I think."

And so saying – clearly unaware of Jonathan's anger – Lord Harrogate turned on his heel and made his way directly towards the lady in question, leaving Jonathan to force down his ire and wonder silently just why he felt so strongly in the first place.

CHAPTER SIX

"Lord Thornley appeared to be most interested in your company!"

Deborah smiled softly but did not reply. There had been a strange array of emotions for her to comprehend the previous evening, but she certainly had enjoyed the company of one or two gentleman in particular.

"And Lord Harrogate!" Lady Havisham exclaimed, clapping her hands together. "He is a great friend of Lord Havisham and whilst I do not know much of his character, I–"

She stopped, turning as the door opened.

"Ah, Havisham! We were just about to discuss your friend. Mayhap you would be good enough to grace us with your presence for just a few minutes?"

All too aware of how Lord Havisham frowned, Deborah sighed inwardly and turned her head away. No doubt the gentleman would have many better things to do than spend time with his mother and would have some excuse as to why he would not oblige them.

Lord Havisham cleared his throat.

"Are you speaking of Lord Harrogate?"

A little surprised, Deborah glanced at him.

"We are!" Lady Havisham cried, still seemingly delighted at the success of the previous evening. "I was informing Miss Fullerton that you consider him to be a very close friend which, of course, must speak of his good character."

Lord Havisham shot a quick look towards Deborah, but she turned her head away, just waiting for his dismissive answer. After what he had said to her – indirectly, of course – the previous evening, Deborah had very little by way of kind consideration for him.

"Lord Harrogate is a gentleman I would consider to be a very close friend, certainly." Coming a little more into the room, he paused as he glanced at Deborah. "However, I would not allow him to court Miss Fullerton, if that is what you are proposing, mother."

Deborah closed her eyes. There was no surprise in her heart upon hearing those words. In fact, part of her had expected them.

"Lord Harrogate is a Viscount, is he not?" Lady Havisham sounded a little confused, but Deborah merely drew in and then let out a long, slow breath, finding herself just as she had been only a few moments before Lord Havisham had entered. Of course, he would not think her a suitable match for his friend, even *if* she were the daughter of a Viscount and Lord Harrogate himself carrying the title of Viscount!

"He is."

"Then, what can be your concern?"

There was nothing but silence to answer Lady Havisham's question and, as Deborah turned her attention back to the gentleman in question, she saw him shifting from foot to foot, his brow furrowed and his lips tugging to one side.

She rose.

"I shall take my leave, if you will excuse me."

Bobbing a quick curtsey, she made her way to the door, only to be prevented by a word from Lady Havisham.

"Wait, my dear, if you please. I am sure that my son will soon enlighten us as to the reason he believes Lord Harrogate to be so unsuitable. A fact which, I confess, I cannot yet understand."

Tilting her head, she lifted one eyebrow in question and Deborah looked back steadily at Lord Havisham, waiting for him to explain himself.

No explanation came.

Lord Havisham rubbed his chin and then gave a small shake of his head.

"Is it not enough to say that I think him unsuitable? I do not consider it important for me to go into particular detail."

A fire began to smolder within Deborah's chest. It seemed that, whilst Lord Havisham had taken on his mother's reprimand about speaking callously, his view of her was entirely unchanged.

"You will not tell us?"

"I do not think it necessary. My warning should be enough."

The fire blew into flame.

"I shall depart so that you might speak openly to Lady Havisham, my Lord." Deborah dropped into a long, lingering curtsey, a little sarcasm creeping into her voice. "I should not like to overhear you inform Lady Havisham that you consider someone such as I – with no dowry to speak of and forced into employment as a companion – would be entirely unsuitable as a match for Lord Harrogate."

Lord Havisham frowned.

"Miss Fullerton, there is no need –"

"I am well aware of your opinion of me, Lord Havisham." The fire within her was burning hotter and hotter and Deborah was all too aware that she was speaking inappropriately but could not hold herself back. "You made that very clear to me last evening. I appreciate that Lord Harrogate is your dear friend and that you should not wish to have him connected to someone such as I, therefore you need not go into particulars. I can assure you that, should the near impossible situation come about where he might show the faintest of interest in my company, I will turn away from it without hesitation. I do hope that satisfies you."

She did not linger to hear his response, all too aware of the shock expressed in Lady Havisham's wide eyes and ajar mouth but turned and quit the room without another word.

THE GARDEN WAS RATHER BEAUTIFUL, Deborah had to admit. She had been wandering through here for the last few minutes, breathing out the anger which still smoked within her. The words he had thrown at her last evening still rang around in her mind and she had no doubt that Lord Havisham's hesitation to speak had only fueled her anger still further. Deborah was all too aware that she had spoken out of turn and with very little consideration for her position within Lord Havisham's household, but she had been entirely unable to hold it within herself any longer. She did not need to be told of how low a position Lord Havisham considered her to be in – he had already made that very clear indeed.

Seeing the small wooden bench by the wall of roses, Deborah sank down carefully, making sure not to let her skirts catch on the thorns. Closing her eyes, she let out a small sigh, realizing just how tense the atmosphere would be between herself and Lord Havisham the next time they met.

"Miss Fullerton."

Her eyes flew open, and she caught her breath. Somehow, Lord Havisham had discovered her and now stood only a few steps away, his hands clasped behind his back and his chest puffed out. His eyebrows were low, and a line had formed between them, making him appear rather foreboding.

Her stomach dropped and she made to rise. Whilst Deborah believed that her anger had been justified, the awareness now of just how upset Lord Havisham was over her response finally struck her. Could he dismiss her? Would he inform his mother that her impertinence would not be tolerated and thus, return Deborah to her father? Just what would become of her then?

"You need not stand, Miss Fullerton." His voice was low, and Deborah sank back onto the bench, keeping her gaze at his feet rather than up at his face. She found her courage suddenly lacking, and was unable to look into his eyes. "Miss Fullerton, there are some things that I must say to you." Her eyes closed tightly, a tremor running down through her. "Might I –" The hesitation in his voice had her head lifting, her eyes opening. "Might I sit by you, Miss Fullerton?"

Astonishment caught her tongue, and it was all she could do to nod. In a moment, Lord Havisham had changed from the angry, frustrated gentleman to one who now appeared to be deeply uncertain. His eyebrows had lifted, his frown had smoothed, and it now seemed that *he* was the one unable to look at her. His eyes were shifting from left to right, never once landing on her, and certainly not lingering on her either. When he sat down, Deborah was aware of the heat of his body, so close to hers, as well as the rippling tension which seemed to run in waves from the top of her head to her toes.

She curled her fingers up tightly together, one hand over the other. The few silent seconds were almost impossible for her to endure, and on three separate occasions, she opened her mouth to speak, only to close it again when she realized that she had nothing she could really say.

"I..." Lord Havisham cleared his throat and closed his eyes tightly for a moment, his lips pulling into a flat line. "Miss Fullerton, I have not been fair." Looking at her, he spread his hands. "I am all too aware of my words, Miss Fullerton. You have judged me just as I deserved." Deborah blinked in confusion, having very little understanding of what he meant. "I can see that I have perplexed you." Sighing, Lord Havisham ran one hand over his eyes, then dropped it back onto his lap. "Miss Fullerton, when it comes to Lord Harrogate and my reluctance to permit him to court you, I can assure you that it has nothing to do with your standing."

A small, disbelieving laugh fled from her lips before Deborah could prevent it and she lowered her head immediately in embarrassment.

"You do not believe me but, as I have said, I can well understand your difficulty. You have judged me just as I deserve. I have not made you welcome in this house. I have not acknowledged your presence often and have been rude enough not to even greet you. My mother is right; I have been harsh and unkind." He took in a deep breath as though it had taken him a great deal of strength to say such a thing. "The reason I did not wish to discuss Lord Harrogate, Miss Fullerton, is not at all what you believe. Rather, it is quite the opposite." His lips tugged gently as she lifted one eyebrow, unconvinced. "Lord Harrogate has been my acquaintance and my friend for many years. Believe me when I tell you that he is *not* a gentleman you ought to consider."

Trying desperately to remove the tightness from her throat, Deborah lifted her chin a notch, hoping she appeared calm and steady.

"And why should that be, Lord Havisham? If it is not because of my lowly status, then what else might the matter be?"

"It has naught to do with you!" Much to her astonishment, Lord Havisham practically threw himself out of his seat, his arms gesticulating furiously. "It is Lord Harrogate who concerns me!"

At this, Deborah's eyes widened in utter astonishment as Lord Havisham ran one hand over his face and then threw his head back for a moment, gazing up to the sky.

"Lord Harrogate seeks a wife who will not be concerned by his continued dalliances and the like," he finished, eventually looking back at her, his hands now falling to his sides. "As much as I have not shown you the respect that I ought, I fear that Lord Harrogate would treat you all the worse. That is not something I cannot have on my conscience, as weak and as useless as it might be at present." The tightness in Deborah's throat returned with such force that she could not even swallow. All that she had flung at Lord Havisham suddenly came back upon her shoulders, pushing her down with both shame and utter mortification. She had not given him the opportunity to explain himself, and had ended up believing the very worst about his character, although it was not as though she had reason not to do so. "You are not to blame yourself, Miss Fullerton. I only wish to assure you that it was naught to do with your current standing as regards Lord Harrogate but simply because his character is not what a gentleman's ought to be."

Deborah could not look at him. Her face burned and her fingers twisted together.

"Thank you, Lord Havisham."

"And I – for my part, Miss Fullerton, will make certain not to speak to you without respect and consideration." His voice dropped a little. "I confess that I have been unkind and thoughtless and for that, I do beg your forgiveness."

The ache in her throat grew, but Deborah forced words to her lips.

"But of course."

There was only a whisper there, but it was enough for Lord Havisham to hear. He nodded stiffly, then turned away, as if to walk back into the house.

"I – I do hope that there will be no more awkwardness between us, Miss Fullerton. I should like to improve your consideration of me."

Dragging her eyes to his, Deborah gave him a small, tight smile that flickered across her face and was gone at the very next moment.

"There is no need for such concern, my Lord. I am sure that –"

"Pray, refer to me as 'Havisham', if you would." His face colored and he cleared his throat. "Forgive me, I have interrupted you. But I do not wish there to be any condescension nor deference. You are the daughter of a Viscount, Miss

Fullerton, and will be treated as such, as you ought to have been from the very moment of your arrival."

A little flummoxed at such a change in Lord Havisham's behavior as well her lingering embarrassment over her previous outburst – which she now realized had not been merited, Deborah could only nod and attempt to smile. There was now a strange tension between them which she feared would take a long time to dissipate but she supposed that it was a little better than the resentment and frustration which she had felt towards him thus far.

"Good." For a moment, it looked as though he wished to say something more, for he shuffled his feet and opened his mouth, only to snap it shut once more. Deborah licked her lips and struggled to find something more to say, her fingers tight together. "Good afternoon, Miss Fullerton."

She tried to smile.

"Good afternoon."

Lord Havisham nodded, straightened his shoulders, gave her a small bow, and then walked away, leaving Deborah with nothing more than the gentle rustling of leaves and sweet birdsong to accompany her whirling thoughts.

CHAPTER SEVEN

The realization that he had been behaving very poorly towards Miss Fullerton had brought with it the uncomfortable sensation that he had been rather selfish of late. Striding along the pavement, Jonathan's brow furrowed as he considered his character, wondering just how it was that Miss Fullerton viewed him. He had attempted to apologize to her, and was quite certain that he had done a very poor job of it indeed. What she had said to him had been quite incorrect as regarded his reasons for pushing her away from Lord Harrogate but, after she had departed, it had taken his mother's gentle questions to make him accept that Miss Fullerton had every reason to think such things of him.

And that, in turn, had given him cause to reconsider his standing in front of Miss Fullerton as it was at present, as well as to think of his own character.

She did look remarkably pretty

Giving himself a stern yet silent rebuke, Jonathan thrust aside all memories of Miss Fullerton sitting out on the garden bench and tried to focus his thoughts on other, more important things. Having just been to his solicitors to organize one or two important matters, Jonathan intended to stop at White's for a short while before returning home. No doubt it would be quiet, but that was precisely what he required at this present moment. He could have a little peace at his own townhouse if he chose to hide away in his study or the library but, even then, the awareness that his mother and Miss Fullerton were present was still something of a distraction – particularly if they were to receive any visitors that afternoon.

Or gentleman callers.

That thought had a weight landing in the pit of his stomach, making him grimace.

You must stop being ridiculous, he told himself firmly. *Miss Fullerton requires a husband and thus, gentleman callers are to be expected!*

His grimace did not lift. Part of him feared that she would be courted by gentlemen of the same ilk as Lord Harrogate, and might eventually end up wed to such a despicable fellow, but then he comforted himself with the knowledge that both he and his mother would make certain that would never occur.

"And why should you take such an interest in her wellbeing?" he muttered to himself, narrowing his eyes as the sunlight blazed across the sky.

There was no reason for him to have any strong consideration for the lady. This Season was meant to be one of nothing but enjoyment on his part, and he did not need to burden himself with any cares or concerns as regarded the young companion. In fact, ought he not to be grateful that his mother was entirely caught up with Miss Fullerton's future, rather than worrying about her son? With Miss Fullerton present, Jonathan had not heard a single word from his mother regarding his status as a bachelor, and that ought to bring him both relief and contentment.

So why were his thoughts still so caught up with the lady? They should be settled on his enjoyments rather than on someone so insignificant to him.

"Oh, Lord Havisham! Lord Havisham!"

It took Jonathan a moment to realize that someone was calling his name. Turning his head, he saw none other than Lady Vivian waving at him from where she sat on a large woolen blanket, with her skirts around her legs and only the very tips of her toes showing. Two other young ladies sat with her, but none of them were waving nor even looking at him. Their eyes were averted, and Jonathan was sure that he saw a flush of pink in one of the other ladies' cheeks. It seemed that they were a little embarrassed by Lady Vivian's loud display.

Sighing inwardly, for he would have much preferred to make his way through the park without interruption, Jonathan demanded silently that he smile before making his way towards her.

The lady did not rise.

"Would you like to join us, Lord Havisham?"

Lady Vivian's eyes were bright, her smile dazzling, but Jonathan's reluctance remained.

"Alas, I cannot. I am already engaged elsewhere." The half-truth was easily spoken, for Jonathan had no intention of lingering for long. "It is a very pleasant day, however. I do hope that you are all enjoying the sunshine."

He smiled at the other two ladies, recognizing them both but struggling to recall their names.

"We are indeed," the second replied, a small smile on her lips but her eyes darting away. "And have you decided to take the air this afternoon?"

"Of course he has, since he is out walking!" Lady Vivian exclaimed, waving a hand at her friend who immediately dropped her head, blushing furiously. "You cannot linger for even a few minutes, Lord Havisham?" Her tone became a little wheedling, and Jonathan shook his head, all the more disinclined towards her company. How much he regretted giving her that ridiculous compliment when they had been at that evening soiree! Clearly that had encouraged her to believe that he very much wanted her company when the opposite was quite true.

"Then mayhap I can enjoy your company instead?" Lady Vivian was not about to be dissuaded it seemed, for she rose and, brushing down her skirts gently, lifted her head and smiled at him. "My mother will not mind, so long as I only walk a short distance. And I am sure that my friends will accompany us so that I am able to return with them once you are to continue on your way."

Unable to do anything but agree, Jonathan offered his arm to her which, after a warm smile up into his eyes, the lady accepted. He fell into step with her and began to walk along the path. Struggling to think of what he might say, he chose to wait for Lady Vivian to speak rather than begin a slightly awkward conversation. After all, that was what had caused him so much difficulty the last time!

"I do hope you are well, Lord Havisham?"

"Very well, I thank you. And you?"

Lady Vivian nodded.

"I confess I have been a little surprised to see Miss Fullerton in company again." Jonathan closed his eyes and resisted the urge to groan aloud. He had only just removed the lady from his thoughts and now Lady Vivian was bringing her back to his mind! "I had thought that she was your mother's companion only and would not often be seen in society." As he considered how he might answer, it took Jonathan a moment to realize that the lady did not need him to respond and was instead continuing to speak without hesitation. "I have asked a few of my friends but *none* of them have heard of the daughter of Lord Ingleby, which is very strange indeed. And to think that she is being considered as a possible match for some of the gentlemen in our society!" The light, tinkling laugh did nothing to bring Jonathan any mirth and he found himself frowning instead – which Lady Vivian did not appear to notice. "I should think that any gentleman who would consider Miss Fullerton would have to have reason to marry such a creature. They might be a little old and seeking a young wife, or mayhap they would do so to avoid scandal! Regardless, I am not convinced that the lady will have any success, although mayhap she too will wish to marry quickly."

"I think you are a little harsh in your considerations, Lady Vivian." His voice was a little hard, but Jonathan did not care. Lady Vivian had spoken too long on the subject of Miss Fullerton, and it was becoming rather wearying. "Miss Fullerton has every reason to make a good match and I do hope that she is able to do so soon."

Lady Vivian's smile shattered, and her eyes narrowed as she looked up at him.

"You speak in very clear terms as regards Miss Fullerton, I think."

"My mother thinks very highly of her, and I have come to realize that her judgments about Miss Fullerton's character are not at all misplaced."

Jonathan did not make any further comment, ignoring Lady Vivian's hard look.

"Goodness." Lady Vivian's quiet remark needled Jonathan and he found himself eager to remove himself from her company. "I do not think I should be at all surprised if I were to see you dancing with Miss Fullerton at the next ball, Lord Havisham!"

A tight knot tied itself in Jonathan's stomach.

"I have no reason to pull back from such a thing, should it be required of me."

Keeping his voice steady, he tried to smile at her, but it would not quite stick.

"Even though there is such a mystery surrounding her?" Lady Vivian asked, sounding astonished. "Have you any understanding as regards Lord Ingleby's silence on even having a daughter?"

Jonathan turned a little, coming to a stop. He had no time for such questions and did not want to even attempt to answer them. For whatever reasons – reasons he could not understand and did not even want to ask about – Lady Vivian appeared to be quite concerned about Miss Fullerton and seemed to want to push her concerns onto Jonathan himself.

"I think that I must continue on my way, Lady Vivian. Forgive me. It seems that our conversation must come to an end for the present."

Her lips pursed but she did drop her hand from his arm without too much hesitation.

"Very well. Good afternoon, Lord Havisham."

Bowing, Jonathan murmured his farewells both to Lady Vivian and to her friends, who walked a little behind them, before turning on his heel and walking briskly away.

Why does she continually ask about Miss Fullerton?

Shaking his head to himself, Jonathan passed one hand over his eyes, his shoulders dropping gently with relief that he was no longer in the company of Lady Vivian. The questions she had asked about Lord Ingleby still remained in his mind, however, and Jonathan did struggle to remove them from his thoughts. There was something of a mystery when it came to Miss Fullerton's father for, even when he had made a throwaway remark about Lord Ingleby being aware of his daughter's presence in society, both the lady herself and his mother had appeared immediately anxious, with Miss Fullerton looking a little frightened.

And then had come the explanation from his mother about *some* gentlemen being selfish, lacking kindness and consideration and, whilst Jonathan knew that she had been speaking of Lord Ingleby, it had been all too clear that her words were also directed towards him.

"But if it is true that Lord Ingleby does not mention his daughter to anyone, then why is there such concern over his awareness of Miss Fullerton being present here?"

Murmuring to himself, Jonathan flushed in embarrassment as two ladies glanced at him and then at each other, their lips curving into a smile at the gentleman who was clearly speaking to himself. Turning, Jonathan made his way a little more quickly along towards White's, glad when he finally ducked inside.

Letting out a long breath, he went to find a quiet corner where he might simply sit in silence with his thoughts for a short time. He did not want to think about Miss Fullerton, nor about his mother, Lady Vivian, or any other young lady. He just wanted to enjoy being here alone.

"Havisham!"

Jonathan closed his eyes. The silence he sought was hiding from him.

"Well, if you do not want my company, then you need only say so!" Lord Harrogate slapped him hard on the back and Jonathan jolted forward, throwing a scowl at his friend. "Goodness, you are in something of a temper!"

"I am not in a temper," Jonathan declared, ignoring the jibe. "I came merely for a little respite."

Lord Harrogate's brow lifted.

"Respite?"

"I have my mother and Miss Fullerton residing with me at present and have only just now found myself in Lady Vivian's presence for a short while. I thought to have a little time to sit alone."

"Then you do *not* wish for my company." Lord Harrogate grinned but did not appear to be in any way put out. "Pray do not concern yourself with *my* feelings!"

Jonathan rolled his eyes and made to walk away from Lord Harrogate, but his friend stepped a little more in front of him.

"Indeed, I was myself speaking to Lady Vivian only a little earlier this morning," he continued, as Jonathan battled against his frustration. "She is remarkably pretty and, if I might speak openly, quite besotted."

Despite his frustration, Jonathan lifted one eyebrow.

"Besotted?"

"With you!" Lord Harrogate laughed at Jonathan's shocked expression. "She was most concerned about an eligible young lady residing in your house, but I assured her that it would not be for long."

Jonathan raked one hand through his hair, an exasperated breath billowing out between his clenched teeth.

"Is that so?"

"It is. I have even made a bet with Lord Thornley that I shall be the one to capture Miss Fullerton's attentions."

A heavy weight dropped into his stomach.

"I beg your pardon?"

"Only a few minutes ago," Lord Harrogate declared, sounding quite proud of himself. "Lord Thornley is also interested in Miss Fullerton and both he and I argued about who we believed to be the most suitable. Since we could not come to an agreement, a bet was made and now I simply *must* gain Miss Fullerton's affections so that I do not lose! That would be disgraceful, although I can well afford to pay, as you know."

Nausea rolled through Jonathan's stomach and for a few moments, he could not speak. To bet on a young lady's future was more than a little distasteful, and Jonathan could not think well of the idea.

"She will not know of it if that is your concern," his friend said as if he could see Jonathan's thoughts. "And besides which, she is the disgraced daughter of a Viscount, why should she concern herself with being the subject of a bet?"

Jonathan frowned.

"Disgraced?"

Lord Harrogate shrugged.

"I do not know the reasons behind such a thing, but Lady Vivian is quite certain of it. After all, why would a gentleman refuse to acknowledge his daughter if such was not the case?"

"I should be very careful indeed of what Lady Vivian has to say," Jonathan warned, his heart beating a little faster as he realized just how quickly Lady Vivian could ruin Miss Fullerton, should she choose to. "Besides which, the *ton* would not think well of you should you marry Miss Fullerton if such rumors were allowed to spread." With relief, he saw the flicker of concern in Lord Harrogate's eyes. For the moment, at least, Miss Fullerton was protected. "Whatever her father might say or, in this case, refuse to say, that does not detract from Miss Fullerton's status, nor her commendable character. If I were you, I should ignore Lady Vivian entirely."

Lord Harrogate nodded, rubbing his chin.

"You are right," he murmured, as Jonathan snapped his fingers to one of the footmen, ordering a brandy for himself. "I shall be careful. Lady Vivian has something of a dislike for the lady, I think." He grinned and elbowed Jonathan in the side. "A little jealousy, no?"

Jonathan, wearied by his many conversations, merely nodded, and then attempted to move past Lord Harrogate.

"I intend to sit alone for a short while, Harrogate," he said pointedly. "I shall see you this evening."

"But of course." Lord Harrogate grinned and stepped aside, letting Jonathan walk directly past him. "This evening where I am sure, Lady Vivian will be very happy to see you again, also."

A muffled groan slipped from Jonathan's lips as sat down in an overstuffed leather chair. Thus far, this was not the delightful Season he had anticipated. Instead, it seemed to be becoming overly complex, confusing, and frustrating. He did not want to have Lady Vivian chasing after him, nor did he wish for Miss Fullerton to be the subject of a bet between two of his friends!

I wish my mother had never returned to London.

Accepting the glass of brandy from the footman, Jonathan threw it back in one gulp and then ordered another.

Although then I would not have met Miss Fullerton.

Closing his eyes, Jonathan let out another heavy sigh.

This was all becoming very complicated indeed.

CHAPTER EIGHT

"Good afternoon, Lord Thornley. Thank you again for calling." Deborah smiled warmly at the gentleman as she rose from her curtsey. This was the second time that Lord Thornley had come for an afternoon call, and from the sidelong glances which Lady Havisham was sending her way, she clearly thought this was of significance.

"I look forward to seeing you both this evening." Lord Thornley smiled before turning and taking his leave of them. Quietly, Deborah sat back down in her chair and smoothed her skirts over her knees.

"Well, what do you think of Lord Thornley?"

Deborah blushed at Lady Havisham's knowing glance.

"I think him a very kind gentleman."

"I believe he is!" Lady Havisham exclaimed as the door opened again. "Ah, Havisham. You have decided to join us, I see."

She lifted one eyebrow in question as Deborah dropped her gaze. There was still an awkwardness between herself and Lord Havisham, where neither of them appeared to know what to say in front of the other. In the few days since he had come to speak to her in the gardens, that tension had only increased rather than faded, leaving her stomach twisting and her heart beating a little more quickly.

"I passed Lord Thornley upon my arrival." There was no lightness in his voice and the knot in Deborah's stomach tightened all the more. "He came to call, I take it?"

"Yes, he did. Pray do not inform me that Lord Thornley is not a suitable gentleman for Miss Fullerton to consider, else I shall be very cross indeed."

There came a short silence and Deborah lifted her gaze to Lord Havisham's, suddenly feeling a little sick. Surely there was not something questionable about the *second* gentleman who appeared to be interested in her! Lord Havisham caught her gaze and looked into her eyes for some moments. Silence surrounded the three of them and it appeared as though he were considering what to say next, for his jaw tightened and he clasped his hands tightly in front of him.

"No, there is nothing of concern."

Deborah's eyes closed but the nausea in her stomach remained. Lady Havisham was exclaiming that she was very pleased to hear such a thing whilst Deborah herself considered that there was more that Lord Havisham had wished to say but, for whatever reason, he had chosen not to do so.

"I am only grateful for Lord Thornley's willingness to call." Speaking up, she caught both Lady Havisham and Lord Havisham's attention. "You can be quite certain, Lord Havisham, that I would not give any true consideration to any gentleman of the *ton* without being certain of their background and circumstance."

"Nor would I," Lady Havisham declared, lifting her

chin as though she was daring her son to disagree with her. "Lord Thornley appears to be a very considerate fellow at least, but it is only the second time that he has come to call."

A tap at the door came and within a few moments, Deborah found herself sitting quite alone, for both Lord Havisham and his mother had been called away for separate matters. Settling her hands in her lap, she closed her eyes and tried to breathe away the coil of tension that had wound itself around her heart. She had no need for concern. Lord Havisham seemed a little worried about Lord Thornley but, given that there was nothing of importance between herself and that particular gentleman at present, what did it matter?

"Miss Fullerton." Her eyes flew open. "I – I have something I must ask you and whilst it is not my business and you might well find yourself eager to remove yourself from my company, I find that I must ask it." Before she could respond, Lord Havisham had seated himself beside her, turning his body a little more towards hers. Shock lodged itself in her throat and she could only blink up at him in surprise. "You must promise me, Miss Fullerton, that you will tell me if you do not wish to answer." Deborah nodded, her throat tight. She did not think that Lord Havisham had ever sat so close to her before. His green eyes glittered, searching hers with a gentle carefulness that she had never once seen before in all their interactions thus far. "I am not intending impertinence in my question nor seeking to throw doubt on anything that you have said, nor on your standing." His chest lifted in a long breath and Deborah curled her fingers together, tension beginning to ripple down her spine. "I have been informed – and I need not say by who – that your father does not acknowledge you."

"Ah..."

It was as if he had struck her hard in the stomach, for Deborah caught her breath as shock poured into every vein. She could not move, could not speak, hearing the blood roar in her ears.

"I have upset you." Lord Havisham scowled as if angry with himself. "As I have said, the reason I ask is not because —"

"Who informed you of this?"

Before she knew what she was doing, Deborah reached out and grasped Lord Havisham's arm, her fingers curling around his sleeve and brushing against the skin of his wrist. Another shock seemed to spike up her arm, but Deborah ignored it, desperate to hear his answer.

"It – it is not from anyone of significance." Lord Havisham leaned forward, looking back into her eyes as if to try to reassure her. "You need not be concerned, Miss Fullerton. It is not as though the *ton* is going to know of this particular rumor."

It would not be a rumor.

"My father is not a kind gentleman, Lord Havisham. Whilst he does not refuse to acknowledge me, as someone obviously believes, he does have very little time for my company and would prefer it if I spent the remainder of my days elsewhere, away from his household, so that he might forget me almost entirely." Drawing in a breath, she saw the questions burning in his eyes but continued to speak quickly in the hope that his questions would fade. "I have been more than grateful to your mother for her generosity towards me, plucking me from my position in his house, such as it was. I do not intend to cause her any difficulty here in London, however. If such things are being said of me, then —"

"Nothing is being said." His warm hand settled over

hers and Deborah's breath hitched for the second time. "Forgive me for asking such a thing, Miss Fullerton. It is clear that I have upset you unnecessarily. The person who suggested such a thing is doing so for their own reasons, I believe."

"And what would such reasons be?" Her heart was still pounding furiously, but the shock was slowly beginning to fade away. "I am nothing to society."

"You are not insignificant." Lord Havisham's voice was gentle, his eyes warm. "I reprimanded Harrogate –" Stopping dead, he squeezed his eyes closed and scowled. "It is Lord Harrogate, needless to say. But I am certain that he shall not repeat such slander to anyone."

Deborah swallowed three times before she could speak, feeling the tears begin to burn in the back of her eyes. The fact that her father had even been *mentioned* had been difficult enough, but now to know that someone else was speaking of him – and her- was making things very trying indeed.

"Thank you, Lord Havisham. I am sure that you have done your best."

In that, at least, she had confidence. Lord Havisham had shown her a good deal more kindness these last few days and, from when he had come to the garden to apologize, Deborah had recognized a change in his demeanor towards her. She had absolute confidence that whatever it was Lord Havisham said or believed as regarded such rumors, he was telling her the truth. Those words would not be spread throughout London society as she feared.

"Are you quite all right?"

Something touched her cheek and Deborah's eyes flew open, startled, just in time to see Lord Havisham dropping his hand and turning his head away from her. Had his fingers been at her cheek? A fire began to spread its flames up her neck and into her face. Whyever would he do such a thing?

"I – I am." Hating that her voice was barely loud enough for even herself to hear, Deborah lowered her gaze. "I apologize for my reaction."

"You need not."

It took Deborah a moment to realize that she was still grasping his sleeve and that his other hand was back atop her own. The softness in his voice confused her, sending a billowing warmth followed by an icy wind through her. She shivered, and Lord Havisham's eyes caught hers again, a small frown flickering across his brow. Was he just as confused as she at this strange interaction between them?

"There is much I could tell you about my father but, in truth, Lord Havisham, I do not wish to speak of him." Her voice was a little steadier now, but her heart still beat furiously. "He is not a good man."

"I am sorry to hear that." After a moment, he lifted his hand away and she released his sleeve, dragging her hand back to her lap and trying to make sense of the myriad of feelings that had now taken her captive. "I have no wish to become such a person, Miss Fullerton. I do hope that now, you are a little more assured of that."

A small smile crinkled her lips.

"If you are asking me whether or not my view of your character is a little improved, Lord Havisham, then I will answer you in the affirmative."

Lord Havisham chuckled and instantly, the strain which had been present broke apart.

"I am very glad to hear it. That has brought me a great deal of relief, I assure you."

She smiled back at him, the tension in her limbs beginning to fade away.

"I am happy here. Your mother is most kind."

"Yes." His sigh dropped his shoulders. "I believe that my mother has always had good intentions. It is a pity that I did not always see that."

"But I am certain she is glad to be in your company now." There seemed to be a need to reassure him, seemed to be an urge to encourage him somewhat, and Deborah spoke with as much conviction as she could muster. "It is good for her to be with you, Lord Havisham. I know that she has missed you these last few years."

A wry smile twisted his lips.

"Would that I could say the same, Miss Fullerton."

"Might I ask..."

She trailed off, realizing from the moment that she spoke that it was not her place to ask such questions, but Lord Havisham merely nodded.

"Please. Continue."

Deborah hesitated, but the small, warm smile on Lord Havisham's face encouraged her.

"It is not my place to know such things, but I presume that there was a reason for your separating yourself from Lady Havisham?"

Lord Havisham's smile disappeared.

"You wish to know why I have not called nor written these last few years?"

"You have written, I know, but –"

"Sporadically," he interrupted. "I have not been an affectionate son and I will admit that, knowing she had a companion, I took even less concern about my mother. It is not because I thought poorly of her, nor because there was any ill feeling between us, but simply because I did not wish for her to continue pressing her opinions and her considerations into my life."

Deborah nodded slowly, although she had to admit that she did not fully understand what was meant by his words.

"I realize now that my mother's eagerness to press me in the manner that she did came from her desire for me to be happy, and her concern that I was not."

"You did not understand that at the time?"

He shook his head.

"I did not. I was only concerned with my feelings on the matter and wanted nothing more than to be entirely on my own. Thus, I avoided my mother for some time. It has only been upon her return that I have come to see the truth of her motivations and, in doing so, have struggled with my own sense of selfishness."

There was no easy response to such a statement, and Deborah tried to find something to say, something which might reassure him, but found herself only smiling gently rather than saying a single word. There was, she realized, a sense of openness between them now, which she had not expected. Because he had come to speak to her in such a gentle and considerate manner, Deborah had found herself telling him a little more about her father than she had intended and he, in turn, was now beginning to respond in kind.

"I think it is wrong for your father to wish to remove you from his house, Miss Fullerton." Butterflies began to beat their wings within her at the gentleness in Lord Havisham's voice. "I cannot imagine that it is due to anything you have done and thus, I must assume that you are suffering under his lack of interest in you."

Her eyes closed for a moment as she took in a deep breath.

"It can be trying, Lord Havisham, certainly." Opening her eyes, she gave him a sad smile. "But I have found the importance of being grateful for what has followed thereafter, Lord Havisham, and thus, I feel that I cannot complain."

He shook his head and ran one hand over his forehead.

"You are a great example, Miss Fullerton."

Recalling how inappropriately she had spoken to him, Deborah laughed, causing Lord Havisham's eyes to flare in surprise.

"After how I have behaved in your company at times, I am surprised you think so."

Laughing, Lord Havisham grinned back at her, his eyes dancing with mirth.

"I do not hold such things against you, Miss Fullerton. There is something quite attractive about a young lady who has the strength of character to speak her mind upon occasion, regardless of whether or not what she says is found to be correct!" Deborah blushed, but could not keep the smile from her face. When his fingers touched hers, she did not pull away. It felt as though it was the right thing to do at this present moment. "I am glad that you are here *and* that my mother is here also." Lord Havisham leaned a fraction closer, and Deborah caught the scent of citrus, her blush growing all the more. "But if there is anything that I can do which would be of assistance to you by way of your father, or your situation with him at present – or if you should even wish to merely discuss it with myself, then please know that I am always more than willing to speak with you. I pray that you continue to be certain of my trustworthiness, Miss Fullerton."

It was a very generous offer and Deborah's heart lifted as she smiled.

"Thank you, Lord Havisham. There is naught that can be done, nor than needs to be done, as regards my father at present but should there be any alteration in my circumstances, you can be sure that I will be willing to come to speak with you about it. It is of benefit to me that my father does not care one whit for London society and will do all he can to avoid any talk of the Season."

"I am glad that you have confidence in me." His fingers tightened around hers and, much to Deborah's surprise, he lifted her hand. When he bowed his head, she assumed that he was merely going to bow over her hand – a kind gesture indeed – but when his lips brushed her skin, Deborah lost all sense. Heat seared her skin and blood roared in her ears, rendering her entirely speechless. Lord Havisham smiled and set down her hand before rising to his feet. She knew that she ought to rise also, ought to give him a curtsey and thank him for his time, but she could not. There was a delicate tremble running through her that made such things seem entirely impossible. "Good afternoon, Miss Fullerton. Thank you for your willingness to speak to me today."

Deborah managed a small nod but nothing more. With wide, astonished eyes, she watched Lord Havisham as he turned on his heel and walked from the room, her heart still beating furiously. She still felt the imprint of his lips on her skin, but as she looked down at her hand, a soft smile pulled at her mouth. Something significant had taken place between them, and Deborah was glad of it. There was no tension, no awkwardness, nothing that could now trouble them. Instead, there seemed to be this strange, lingering uncertainty as to what it was that she now felt for Lord Havisham, but that did not trouble Deborah one whit. Instead, she could only smile, glad that, for the moment, things were a little more settled between them.

CHAPTER NINE

There he is.
    Jonathan cleared his throat, lifted his chin, and then made his way directly towards Lord Thornley.

"Good evening." He bowed just as Lord Thornley's eyes turned towards him. "I do apologize for interrupting your conversation."

"No, not at all. I was merely finishing a conversation with Lord Tenton about his estate."

Jonathan smiled briefly.

"I see."

"I am sure that –"

"I have come to speak with you about Lord Harrogate."

Lord Thornley's mouth closed slowly as he studied Jonathan. A line formed as he frowned, and a new tension appeared around his mouth.

"Indeed."

"There is a bet, I understand."

Jonathan was all too aware that such bets were not his business, but after his conversation with Miss Fullerton some two days ago, he had found himself troubled with the knowledge of such a bet. The urge to protect her was significant indeed, and Jonathan now found that he could not prevent himself from speaking so.

Lord Thornley's frown grew.

"There is, yes, but I cannot understand –"

"Miss Fullerton is under the care of my mother and thus, under my supervision also," Jonathan stated, making himself as plain as could be without going into specific details. "I am aware that she is both my mother's companion and also a young lady in her own right and standing. However, I must make certain that any potential suitor has the right intentions towards her."

Lord Thornley's expression did not change.

"I am a little surprised that you would take this much of an interest in the lady, Havisham."

"My mother is very fond of her." That was true and whilst it was not the real explanation for why Jonathan had so much interest in what happened to Miss Fullerton, it was an easy enough response. "Now, about this bet. I –"

"That would be your friend, Lord Harrogate." Lord Thornley rolled his eyes. "He is quite determined that he will win the lady and was eager to have me place a bet."

"You did not need to agree."

Lord Thornley sucked in a breath, then let it out slowly.

"I suppose I did not, but the arrogance of the gentleman forced me to agree. I could not permit him to continue speaking with such breathtaking conceit without response."

Jonathan scowled and looked away. That was, he supposed, a reasonable response. Lord Harrogate was as Lord Thornley described him, although such traits had never concerned Jonathan before now. Perhaps they had been too similar in that regard.

"I am afraid that I cannot remove myself from that bet, Lord Havisham."

"I am aware of that." Jonathan spoke with a little more force than he had intended. "Is it a significant sum?"

Tilting his head to one side, Lord Thornley cast his eyes up to the ceiling.

"It is not *insignificant,* but neither is it an amount which I could not pay, if you understand me."

"You would have no difficulty doing so."

Lord Thornley shook his head.

"But I do not wish to lose, however."

"You should like to wed Miss Fullerton?"

Much to Jonathan's surprise, Lord Thornley's eyes widened and, a few moments later, he began to laugh.

"Wed?" he spluttered, as though Jonathan had said the most ridiculous thing. "That is not the bet, Lord Havisham! I should never have made such a bet! Whatever has Lord Harrogate told you?"

Jonathan blinked rapidly, trying to understand what Lord Thornley meant.

"I was sure that Lord Harrogate informed me that it was whoever managed to wed the lady would..." Closing his eyes, he did not finish his sentence as the exact words Lord Harrogate had said to him came back to his mind. "It is not about matrimony."

"No, indeed not!" Lord Thornley exclaimed, still chuckling. "It is about gaining her affections rather than her hand."

A small bubble of anger revealed itself in Jonathan's core, but he did not acknowledge it. The truth had stunned him, to the point that he had very little idea of what he ought to do next. *What will Miss Fullerton think?*

"I thought you were interested in her."

"I was, certainly, and still think her a very fine young lady, but there is a difficulty with continuing any such connection, given that she has no dowry and, quite frankly, I could do better than a mere companion who has been allowed a little more freedom than most."

Jonathan's stomach turned over as fire began to line his veins. These two gentlemen were not giving any thought to the young lady herself but were rather thinking only of all that they might gain from her. If one managed to obtain her affections, then the bet would be won, and they would win a significant sum from the other. What became of Miss Fullerton thereafter did not appear to be of their concern.

"And what happens if the young lady gives her affections to another entirely?" he managed to ask, aware of the darkness in his voice. "What say you then?"

Lord Thornley shrugged.

"Then the bet is at an end and we both must concede that we have failed."

Jonathan nodded slowly, one hand curling up tightly. He wanted very much to go in search of Miss Fullerton and tell her the truth of the matter, but at the same time, he did not wish to do anything which would harm her – and that would harm her greatly, he was sure.

"I see."

"This does not displease you, I hope?" Lord Thornley gave another laugh, but it was, this time, rather awkward. "It is only a small matter."

"It will not be a small matter to her."

Lord Thornley lifted one shoulder.

"Miss Fullerton will not be injured in any severe way. Society will not become aware of the bet and, given that her reputation will not be damaged, I cannot see any issue with our bet, as it stands."

Jonathan bit his lip before he spoke.

"I am not pleased with such a bet. You must end it." Lord Thornley's eyes flared wide in surprise, but Jonathan stood his ground. "At once. She is my mother's companion, and I will not have any hint of embarrassment brought to her for fear it will damage my mother's reputation."

It was not the truth, certainly, but it was enough of an explanation as to make his complaint reasonable.

"I hardly think that is fair." Tilting his head to one side, Lord Thornley studied Jonathan as though he were seeing him for the first time. "A bet in White's Betting Book cannot simply be destroyed, as you well know."

Jonathan let his breath hiss out between his teeth, already frustrated. Given that he himself had, in the past, made a good many bets, it was foolish to have any expectation that it would simply be brought to an unfulfilled end.

"I have already attempted to dissuade Miss Fullerton from Lord Harrogate, however," he said quickly, hoping that this might bring the matter to a close. "The bet is unfairly weighted towards your success because I have done so."

Lord Thornley shrugged, although his lips curved in a triumphant smile. Jonathan scowled for it seemed the man was not to be moved from his position. The bet, to his mind, was utterly distasteful, for it attempted to toy with Miss Fullerton's affections. However, to let Lord Thornley know of such particular concerns would, no doubt, have consequences for himself and for the lady. Lord Thornley would have no hesitation in telling others in society that Lord Havisham was attempting to defend his mother's companion which, in turn, would bring various questions to the fore.

"You will not say anything *further* to Miss Fullerton, I hope?" Lord Thornley nudged Jonathan, a broad grin on his face which Jonathan found most unpleasant. "I have taken you into my confidence and, should it be discovered that you have informed Miss Fullerton of the particulars of our bet, then I think it only fair that *you* pay us both the required sum."

Jonathan snorted.

"I hardly think that fair."

"All the same, I do not expect anything to be betrayed," Lord Thornley warned. "Come now, you are not a gentleman who has any concerns but his own. I cannot see how this would trouble you!"

The knife to his heart twisted as Jonathan realized that, had he been informed of this only a few weeks ago, he would have found nothing objectionable about the affair whatsoever. It was only because it concerned Miss Fullerton that he now took umbrage with the matter.

And it is only because Miss Fullerton has made you aware of your own selfishness with regard to your mother and, indeed, your attitude towards herself also.

"You are bound by a gentleman's honor not to speak of this bet to Miss Fullerton," Lord Thornley finished, sounding triumphant. "And I should not like you to become the subject of scorn within society. That would be most unpleasant."

Jonathan's heart lurched as a cold sheen ran over his skin.

"I do not understand –"

"Lord Harrogate is a *most* disloyal fellow," Lord Thornley sighed, although his lips curved into a grim smile. "When he is in his cups, he speaks of the most astonishing things – including one particular incident with a Lady Ensley."

Jonathan's blood turned to ice as he narrowed his gaze but Lord Thornley only grinned.

"Whatever he has told you, that is naught more than a fabrication," he stated, firmly. "To believe a gentleman so in his cups is ridiculously foolish."

Lord Thornley shrugged.

"I am certain that there is *some* truth to be acknowledged there. And whether or not it is true, you must know that the *ton* will be very glad to hear of any such rumor. You will be unable to escape it." His hands curling tight into fists, Jonathan took a step forward, but Lord Thornley only laughed, knowing that Jonathan was bound by the threats he had just now set before him. There was nothing for him to do but accept that he could not tell Miss Fullerton about this particular bet, even though every single part of him wanted to do so at once. "Ah now, we are to be interrupted – and just at the right time too." Lord Thornley turned away from Jonathan and bowed low. "Good evening, Lady Vivian, Lady Catherine. I do hope that you are both well this evening?"

Jonathan wanted to groan aloud but he forced his hands to relax. He did not want to be in Lady Vivian's company, but now that she was here, he would, no doubt, have to ask her if she wished to dance and thereafter, sign her dance card. He had made that promise to her, after all, and it was only reasonable that she should expect such a thing from him.

"Very well." Lady Vivian turned to Jonathan with an expectant smile, one eyebrow lifting gently. "And you, Lord Havisham?"

"I have had a pleasant evening thus far," Jonathan replied, giving both the ladies a small bow whilst sending a sharp glance towards Lord Thornley, who simply ignored him. "I do hope you are well also, Lady Catherine?"

His vague attempt to pull the conversation away from Lady Vivian failed, for the lady touched his arm with the very same bold manner he had seen so often before.

"I do recall, Lord Havisham, that you were eager to dance with me the next time we were in company at a ball." Her smile brightened all the more. "And see, here is my dance card ready for you."

She held it up, dangling it in front of his eyes and Jonathan had no other recourse but to accept it.

"You have not had any other gentlemen eager to dance with you this evening?" he queried, a little surprised at the blank dance card. "That is most astonishing, Lady Vivian. I was certain that I should have very few dances left to choose from."

The lady laughed and again, her hand caught his arm.

"Ah, but you see, I have refused them all so that *you* might have the very first choice." A gleam came into her eyes and Jonathan's stomach began to churn, fearing now that the lady thought he held her in some sort of affection. "Am I not kind and *most* considerate?"

"Indeed."

There was nothing else for him to say, and he quickly scribbled his name down for the quadrille. Handing it back to her, Jonathan caught the flare of disappointment in her eyes as she saw his name written there. Given the shattering of her smile, it was clear that Lady Vivian had expected a great deal more from him – perhaps the waltz or supper dance. But he would not give her more than a single dance.

I cannot encourage any false impression, Jonathan told himself, as he then turned to Lady Catherine. *I must make her aware that I hold her in no greater regard than any other.*

"I was a little surprised to see Miss Fullerton present." Jonathan threw a quick glance towards Lady Vivian before perusing Lady Catherine's dance card. Hers held only three spaces and Jonathan wrote down his name for one of them, so that Lady Vivian would not think herself to be singled out in any way. "I believe she is even going to dance!"

"I believe so," Jonathan murmured, not wishing to be drawn on the subject. He had enough to think about as regarded Miss Fullerton and did not want to contend with more.

"But you are aware that she —"

"Miss Fullerton is my mother's responsibility, Lady Vivian." Turning back towards her, he gave her a quick smile which he hoped would prevent her from any further conversation. "I am quite sure that you will be able to have the rest of your dance card filled very soon, now that I have been fortunate enough to write my name down." Lord Thornley cleared his throat and Jonathan grinned despite his lack of respect for the fellow. Here, at least, Lord Thornley was going to be of some benefit. "Lord Thornley, I believe, is looking rather eager indeed!"

Lady Vivian's smile was less than convincing but she had no other choice but to hand her dance card to the waiting gentleman, who grasped at it eagerly. Having no wish to linger near to Lady Vivian, Jonathan bowed and excused himself, promising that he was looking forward to dancing with both the ladies later on in the evening.

Turning, he walked without purpose through the ballroom, his duty as regarded Lord Thornley unable to be completed. He did not like at all what he had heard from the fellow, for Lord Thornley appeared quite eager just to use Miss Fullerton's gentle heart to win a bet, rather than showing any real care for the lady herself. And then to threaten Jonathan, simply to make safe his bet, added to that picture of complete inconsideration. Grimacing, Jonathan shook his head, not quite certain what he ought to do. He could not tell her the truth about the bet. That would then lead to his having to pay both Lord Thornley *and* Lord Harrogate a significant sum but, more importantly, would have the *ton* all too aware of his involvement in the affair with Lady Ensley, which would cause significant whisperings and rumor if not complete scandal. It would not matter what he said, nor how he defended himself – if the *ton* thought him guilty, then he would be guilty indeed. His brow furrowed. His sole purpose was to protect Miss Fullerton, but he was no longer sure of the best way to go about the matter whilst making certain that his own reputation remained unchanged.

"You have returned to us, I see."

Jonathan's thoughts fled as he lifted his eyes and, to his surprise, saw that he had been wandering towards his mother.

"Given that I have not seen either yourself or Miss Fullerton this evening, I hardly think I have *returned,* mother."

Lady Havisham rolled her eyes.

"You need not be so pedantic." Her eyes narrowed gently. "Are you come to inform me that Miss Fullerton should not be dancing? I should remind you that –"

"You already informed me that you had every intention of encouraging Miss Fullerton to dance this evening and I have no objection," Jonathan reassured her before she could begin to pile burning coals onto his head and shoulders. "I do hope that all is well?" Much to his surprise, his mother did not smile in response as he had expected. Instead, her frown grew, and she shook her head. "Mother?"

Letting out a heavy sigh, she spread her hands.

"There are only one or two gentlemen seeking Miss Fullerton out for a dance, but I am not at all convinced that either would be suitable. If Lord Thornley might only make his way over, then..."

Trailing off, she looked away and Jonathan followed the very same direction of her gaze – only for his breath to catch in his chest.

Miss Fullerton was returning to them arm in arm with a gentleman Jonathan only vaguely knew. However, it was not that awareness which made him gasp, but rather the sheer beauty of Miss Fullerton. Even in a simple gown with very little embellishment, Jonathan found her beauty to be entirely unmatched. Her cheeks glowed, her eyes sparkled and the way her dark hair shimmered in the light demanded his attention.

Something akin to envy rose in his chest and Jonathan allowed it to fill him. The moment she was back by his mother's side, he bowed and greeted her warmly, relieved when the other gentleman took his leave.

"I do hope you are having a pleasant evening?"

"I am."

Her eyes strayed from his, turning to the left and then to the right although Jonathan did not know who she could be looking for.

"And have you danced often?"

Her gaze returned to him, but her smile faded.

"I have only been claimed for a few dances, Lord Havisham."

A small line drew itself between her brows, as if she were waiting for him to make some disdainful remark.

"Well, that is excellent!" His exclamation made her frown grow all the more, now confused by his exuberance.

"Might I be able to add to your dance card?" The moment the question was out of his mouth, Jonathan knew that he had made a mistake. Miss Fullerton's eyebrows shot up into her hair and even his mother turned to face him with an expression of astonishment. "I think it might encourage some of the other suitable gentlemen of the *ton* to come and consider you," he added lamely, knowing full well that it was not the reason he had asked Miss Fullerton to dance. "That is, only if you would wish to dance with me, Miss Fullerton?"

She blinked rapidly and did not answer him for some moments. Then, without a word, she slipped off her dance card from her wrist and handed it to him, letting Jonathan peruse it without hesitation. When he glanced up at her, he saw all too clearly the concern which widened her eyes. Clearly, she was afraid that he would think the few names on her dance card to be very embarrassing indeed.

His heart twisted and before he could prevent himself, Jonathan had written his name down for the cotillion and, secondly, the waltz.

What am I doing?

It was there now, and he could not take it back. Handing her the dance card, he tried to smile but struggled to do so, a little worried about her reaction, also. Miss Fullerton's eyes flared, and she looked from the dance card to his face and then back again, as if she were attempting to make sure that this was what he wanted.

Lady Havisham leaned over and let out a small exclamation.

"Good gracious! The waltz?" Her eyes turned back to Jonathan, and he merely shrugged, trying not to let that particular remark embarrass him. "My goodness, Havisham," his mother continued. "You truly are attempting to bring Miss Fullerton some attention, are you not?"

"I am sure I will succeed," Jonathan replied, as Miss Fullerton's cheeks glowed with a rosy blush. "But only if you wish it, Miss Fullerton. I do not have to dance the waltz with you if your preference would be to stand back instead."

Her eyes caught his and the swirl of gold and brown in her eyes told him that she had already made up her mind.

"Thank you, Lord Havisham. I would be delighted to dance with you."

Smiling back at her, Jonathan bowed again.

"Then it is the cotillion and the waltz, Miss Fullerton," he told her, as if she was not already aware. "And I am already looking forward to them both."

And that, he realized as Miss Fullerton murmured some compliment in return, was the truth of it. He wanted very much to stand up with Miss Fullerton and to have her tight in his arms.

There was no reasonable or easily understood explanation as to why he felt that way, but Jonathan did not shy away from the truth. He suddenly could not wait for the waltz to begin, so that he might pull Miss Fullerton close and dance with her for all society to see. He did not care what they might say, did not care what whispers would be spoken behind gloved hands. All he wanted was to have Miss Fullerton in his arms as he danced with her.

His anticipation grew with every second which passed for that, he was sure, would be the most singular pleasure of this evening and it could not come soon enough.

CHAPTER TEN

Deborah did not know how she felt. All too aware that she, a companion, was now dancing with an Earl, Deborah struggled to even lift her head to look into Lord Havisham's eyes.

"I am not disappointing you, I hope?"

Her eyes flared in surprise.

"Disappointing me?"

Her words were breathless, such was the exertion which came with being twirled around the room, but Lord Havisham's reply was calm and steady.

"You appear to be a little troubled, Miss Fullerton. Will you not look at me?"

For whatever reason, it took Deborah a great deal of effort to lift her gaze, and, when she finally did so, her heart slammed so hard into her chest that she was forced to catch her breath.

"Dancing with me is not so frightening, I hope?"

"It *is* quite terrifying, Lord Havisham," she managed to reply, unable to hold his gaze steadily. "Not that it is with you, but rather that I am waltzing at all!" At this, Lord

Havisham let out a soft chuckle and Deborah managed a small smile in return. "I am quite certain that everyone is watching me."

"They might well be, but that is just as we wish it, is it not?"

Deborah's lips twisted to one side, but she did not say a word of response.

"If we are to find you a good match, then you must realize that gentlemen need to be aware of you?" His hand tightened on hers, his other about her waist and Deborah could not find any strength to respond. She was much too aware of him, aware of his strength and his overwhelming presence. Her stomach was churning furiously, her skin burning with heat which did not dissipate, no matter how long she waited. Her mind was filled with thoughts only of Lord Havisham and, whilst she found herself anxious and worried about dancing with him in such a manner, at the same time, Deborah did not want the dance to ever end. "And I must speak to you about Lord Thornley."

At such a change in conversation, Deborah looked back up at him in surprise, seeing the frown now flickering across his brow and the way that his smile had faded.

"Oh?"

He opened his mouth to speak, but at that very moment, the music began to slow, signaling the end of the dance. Lord Havisham grimaced and, much to Deborah's astonishment, tugged her a little closer as though he were entirely reluctant to allow her free of him. Looking up into his face, Deborah held Lord Havisham's gaze for some moments as everything else seemed to fade away. Then the music was at an end and the conversation around them soon quickly began to flow but still, Deborah could not look away. Lord Havisham closed his eyes and let out a long breath which danced across her cheek and sent a swirl of butterflies into her stomach.

"I should return you to my mother." His voice was low, his words dragging out slowly. "I had hoped to speak to you but mayhap..." His lips curved gently, and he slowly released her hand, his other one falling from her waist. "Later this evening or the morrow shall suffice."

Deborah could not speak, but managed a small nod, the butterflies in her stomach still fluttering furiously. Feeling curiously empty now that he had released her from his embrace, she turned and accepted his arm, walking alongside him so that they might return to where Lady Havisham was waiting. The broad smile on the lady's face told Deborah that she believed the evening to have gone very well, and that the dance with Lord Havisham had done exactly as it had intended – but that in itself brought Deborah no pleasure. She only found herself a little disappointed that the waltz was now at an end.

"That was very well done," Lady Havisham murmured, clearly not wishing to make too much of what had taken place. "There was much attention placed on you, Miss Fullerton! I am sure that you will have many gentlemen seeking out your company very soon."

This did not bring Deborah a thrill of delight as she had expected it to, and she struggled to smile. "I am very grateful, I am sure."

"And you, my dear boy!" Lady Havisham put one hand on Lord Havisham's arm, looking up at him with a warm, broad smile. "I am a little surprised at just how well you danced. I was quite certain that you had forgotten how to waltz entirely!"

This teasing made Deborah smile and Lord Havisham chuckle. As he continued to speak to his mother, Deborah found herself a little distracted by a quiet conversation that was taking place behind her, quite certain that she had heard her name mentioned.

"I do not know what Lord Havisham was thinking."

"To stand up with someone so low in status!"

They are talking about me. A quick glance around told her that three young ladies were standing behind her and making very little effort to hide their voices. Her shoulders drooped but Deborah told herself plainly that she did not need to stand and listen to such disparaging remarks. It would only bring her anxiety as well and was taking the joy from the few minutes she had enjoyed in Lord Havisham's arms. Her heartbeat still a little rapid, she leaned forward towards Lady Havisham, begging to be excused for a few moments to refresh herself. Nodding, Lady Havisham was quickly drawn back into conversation and Deborah hurried away, not wanting to linger and hear whoever was talking about either herself or Lord Havisham in such terms. It would not take her long, but by the time she returned, Deborah prayed that the ladies would have moved away or been taken to dance and allow her the rest of the evening free of their unwelcome company.

∽

"I believe that Lord Havisham is quite the bachelor."

Deborah's stomach dropped as she moved forward, stopping a short distance away. The ladies who had been talking of her and Lord Havisham were still present, although there were only two of them now, rather than three.

"Mayhap this Miss Fullerton wishes to try to catch him for herself!"

The laughter that followed sent Deborah's heart spiraling towards the ground.

"She will soon find that *I* am the one who will gain Lord Havisham's full attention," said the first. "He has already shown me significant interest, and I do not think it will take him long to understand just how much he could gain from a connection with me. I will make certain that he understands it, if I must."

The second lady tilted her head, her voice still clear as Deborah took a step closer, wanting now to listen for a little longer. This sounded somewhat concerning and, whilst it was not her business as to whom Lord Havisham took as a bride, Deborah could not help but listen on.

"Make certain?" the second lady asked, a small injection of laughter, running through her voice. "Whatever can you mean?"

A small, quiet laugh came from the first lady.

"There are ways and means of trapping a gentleman, Lady Catherine, even if it does mean soiling my reputation *just* a little."

Deborah's heart turned over in her chest. She did not recognize the lady who was speaking, and yet had no doubt that it was Lord Havisham that she spoke of. Uncertain of what to do, she made to step forward, only for someone to tap her on the shoulder.

Turning, Deborah looked into the face of a young lady she did not know. With fiery red hair and deep blue eyes, the young lady was certainly striking, but did not appear to be overly confident, given the way that she bit her lip.

"Good evening." Deborah tried to smile, wondering why this lady had approached her. "I do not think that..."

"We have not been introduced. I am Miss Judith Newfield."

"Oh." Deborah's small smile faltered. "Miss Deborah Fullerton. I am companion to Lady Havisham."

Miss Newfield nodded.

"Yes, I am aware. I came, Miss Fullerton, to apologize for my friend's remarks, which I am certain you overheard." Her eyes drew towards the two young ladies just beyond Deborah, the ones she had overheard speaking of Lord Havisham. "I am quite certain that they were all too aware of your presence and spoke as they did with the sole intention to harm you. I stood there with them and now feel myself culpable. Therefore, I went in search of you so that I might apologize and, for my part at least, beg your forgiveness."

This was all said in a great rush, the words tumbling out as though she only had a very short time to speak and had to do so at once. A little taken aback, Deborah stammered something incomprehensible and then gave herself a small shake, clearing her throat as she did so.

"You have quite astonished me, Miss Newfield." The young lady dropped her head but the redness in her cheeks, Deborah was sure, came from naught but embarrassment. "But I certainly do appreciate your consideration. However, there is nothing you need apologize for, given that you said nothing at all."

Miss Newfield lifted her head, although her sorrowful expression remained.

"I do not like that they consider you to be a good deal lower than they are," she stated plainly. "If I am to be frank, I believe them a little jealous of your waltz with Lord Havisham."

Deborah's brows lifted.

"But he only did so in order to encourage other gentlemen to consider me." Seeing the way Miss Newfield's eyes rounded, Deborah dropped her gaze, a little embarrassed at having spoken so openly. "I am Lady Havisham's companion, yes, but she is quite determined that I should find a suitable match. I am very blessed indeed."

Miss Newfield's lips twisted.

"My brother insists that I wed this Season also," she replied, sending sympathy spiraling into Deborah's heart. "But it is difficult when I am in the shadow of Lady Vivian and Lady Catherine."

"I think you quite striking," Deborah replied, now beginning to have a sense of solidarity with the young lady and rather touched that she had thought to come to her directly, to apologize for something that she had taken no part in! "I am sure that you will find a good match very soon."

Again, the young lady did not smile, although the frown on her forehead softened somewhat.

"You are very kind. I am hopeful that Lady Vivian will soon find herself betrothed and then I might, perhaps, be able to step forward a little more."

Deborah's stomach tightened.

"Do you know if she has anyone particular in mind?" she asked, stepping a little closer. "It is only that I could not help but overhear some particular remarks as regards Lord Havisham."

Miss Newfield nodded.

"He has shown a particular interest in her, I think. Lady Vivian expects his court very soon."

"Oh." Suddenly, her concern did not seem to be so very important. "I did not realize that Lord Havisham had expressed any eagerness to further their acquaintance." Catching Miss Newfield's slightly lifted eyebrow, Deborah flushed with embarrassment, her chest a little tight. "That is not to suggest that he often shares such things with me, nor that I would expect to be aware of any such preferences."

"Of course." Miss Newfield finally smiled and the tension which had wrapped itself all around Deborah quickly unraveled. "He appears to be a very considerate gentleman."

Deborah laughed.

"I did not always think so, Miss Newfield. Indeed, I believe that Lord Havisham himself would state that he was not at all inclined towards my company when I first arrived, but things are much improved now."

"You think his character has improved?"

Considering this, Deborah tilted her head gently to one side.

"I think that I would state that it has."

"Then it is little wonder that Lady Vivian is so inclined towards him," came the reply. "I shall hope and pray that their courtship will soon take place so that the *ton* will no longer consider her to be eligible – although that is for an entirely selfish reason, I confess."

"I shall not think worse of you for it," Deborah replied, as Miss Newfield smiled for what was now the second time. "Thank you for coming to speak to me, Miss Newfield. You have no need to apologize, I assure you."

"I am glad." Miss Newfield's eyes widened for a moment and then she quickly bobbed a curtsey. "I must beg to be excused. I believe Lady Vivian is now searching for me."

Deborah nodded and did not turn her head to look.

"But of course. Good evening."

Miss Newfield did not reply but quickly moved away, leaving Deborah to stand alone. She did not want to turn back towards Lord Havisham for fear of Lady Vivian becoming aware of her and perhaps realizing that she had overheard some of what was said. Walking away in the opposite direction, Deborah made her way slowly to Lady Havisham, only to see Lord Havisham leading out Lady Vivian to the center of the room.

She stopped. Her heart was suddenly aching, her shoulders drooping and her gut twisting. There was no clear explanation for why she should feel such things, but her eyes remained fixed on Lord Havisham's face and, as he turned to face Lady Vivian, Deborah saw the broad smile settling across his features.

A heavy weight pulled her spirits low.

He will court Lady Vivian.

The thought was a painful one, and Deborah frowned hard, rubbing one hand across her eyes in the hope that it would push away the sight of him dancing with Lady Vivian. These strange feelings were not ones that she welcomed, not ones that she wanted to feel, deep within her heart, and yet, they remained.

Was she jealous?

Closing her eyes, Deborah shook her head to herself.

She was being ridiculous. To have any jealousy over Lady Vivian dancing with Lord Havisham was foolishness indeed. He had danced with her to encourage other gentlemen to do the same and not for any other reason. Mayhap her feelings came solely from her concern over Lady Vivian and her intentions towards Lord Havisham, but given that Miss Newfield had told Deborah of Lord Havisham's interest in Lady Vivian, what was there now to worry her? She ought to be glad that Lord Havisham had an interest in that particular lady, and that Lady Havisham might soon find her son wed, rather than allowing any sort of feelings of envy and upset to trouble her!

"Ah, there you are, Miss Fullerton. I thought I had lost you!"

Seeing the smile on Lady Havisham's face, Deborah berated herself silently for feeling even a hint of envy. If Lady Havisham was happy and Lord Havisham settled on his choice of Lady Vivian, then what right had she to be concerned?

"I was speaking with Miss Newfield," Deborah told her, as Lady Havisham nodded. "I see that Lord Havisham is dancing again."

"Yes." Lady Havisham's smile dimmed for a few moments. "With a Lady Vivian. I do not know her particularly well, I confess, but she certainly seems eager to be in my son's company." A sidelong glance caught Deborah's attention. "Did you see them step out together?"

Heat crawled up Deborah's spine.

"I did." Unwilling to admit – even to herself – that she had been watching Lord Havisham step out, Deborah tried to smile. "It has been a very pleasant evening."

This brought a brightness back into Lady Havisham's face and she reached out to catch Deborah's hand, pressing it gently.

"I am so very glad. And – oh! Good evening, Lord Thornley."

Deborah turned her head just as Lord Thornley dropped into a bow.

"Good evening, Lady Havisham, Miss Fullerton."

A warm smile pulled at his lips and Deborah smiled back at him at once. She liked Lord Thornley. He had always made pleasant conversation and she considered him rather kind given that he was willing to converse and engage with her.

"Good evening, Lord Thornley. I do hope that you have

been enjoying this evening?"

He nodded, his gaze fixing itself to her.

"I am, although it is much improved now that I have you for company."

Heat began to billow out in her chest, spreading warmth up to her neck and into her cheeks. It was not that she found Lord Thornley particularly handsome nor that she was in any way affected by his presence, but merely that she was unused to such compliments. A little embarrassed at her blush, Deborah tried to find something to say to distract Lord Thornley from her current appearance. Thankfully, Lord Thornley continued speaking as though he had not even noticed her flushed cheeks.

"And are you dancing this evening, Miss Fullerton? I was certain that I saw you standing up with Lord Havisham!"

The astonishment in his voice made her blush all the more.

"I was, yes. Lady Havisham has given me permission and –"

"Miss Fullerton is an excellent dancer." Lord Havisham's voice floated towards them, but Deborah dropped her gaze to the floor, already embarrassed by Lord Thornley's exclamation and now additionally by Lord Havisham's interruption. "I have enjoyed her company in two dances this evening thus far."

Lord Thornley grinned, his eyes alight.

"I must hope, then, that you still have one or two dances remaining, Miss Fullerton? I should very much like to enjoy your company in much the same way as Lord Havisham – and given that he cannot dance with you again this evening, *I* shall permit myself to feel a little more delight that such a particular pleasure is still to come for me."

Deborah nodded, still struggling to lift her eyes to either Lord Havisham or Lord Thornley's face.

"But of course."

She slipped off her dance card and made to hand it to Lord Thornley, only for Lord Havisham to frown, reach forward and grasp at her hand.

"Alas, Miss Fullerton is not to dance again this evening."

Her hand fell to her side and heat poured into her face. Whatever was he doing? Was he preventing her from dancing with only Lord Thornley or was this because he believed that she had danced too much already? Perhaps the *ton* were speaking of her, and he did not want to encourage the rumors – but why then ask to waltz with her, knowing it would bring her attention from the other guests?

"Havisham!" Lady Havisham placed both hands on her hips as Lord Thornley began to frown. "You cannot prevent Miss Fullerton from dancing, that is most unkind."

Lord Havisham did not so much as glance at Deborah or his mother, but instead kept his eyes trained on Lord Thornley. His shoulders were a little lifted and his brows pulled tight together as if he were angry with the fellow, although Deborah did not understand why. Shame began to pile itself onto her shoulders as she tried to keep her chin lifted rather than drop it further towards her chest. Whatever Lord Havisham's reasons, she could not have felt any lower in his eyes than she did at present.

"I see that you seek to protect Miss Fullerton." Lord Thornley's eyebrows wiggled but Lord Havisham's expression did not change. "But you need not concern yourself, Havisham. My intentions are true enough, as I am sure you know."

Deborah kept her gaze fixed on Lord Havisham, her

hands curling tightly into fists as tension flooded her. Lord Thornley was practically declaring that he was interested in furthering his acquaintance with her and yet Lord Havisham seemed entirely unmoved. Why was he behaving so? Part of her wanted to step past him and hand her dance card to Lord Thornley without so much as a by-your-leave but, given her position, Deborah knew that she could not show such disrespect. Lady Havisham settled a hand on Deborah's arm, her eyes narrowed as she glared at her son, but he did not relent.

"I will not repeat myself, Lord Thornley, nor will I go into any further discussion on the matter either with yourself or with Miss Fullerton." Lord Havisham's voice was low, his jaw tight. "I do hope I have made myself clear."

Lord Thornley said nothing for some moments. His eyes turned towards Deborah, and, with a heavy sigh, he shrugged.

"I shall wait until next time, Miss Fullerton," he said, unable to find a way to convince Lord Havisham. "Forgive me."

The lump in her throat would not move and Deborah could only nod as tears began to fill her eyes. Blinking rapidly, she tried to remain steady and calm, only to see Lady Vivian standing just behind Lord Thornley. And as the gentleman moved away, Deborah was left staring at Lady Catherine and Lady Vivian as they stood together. Their eyes were bright with laughter, and they made no attempt to hide their mocking smiles. It was apparent that they had overheard everything, and Deborah finally dropped her head as mortification cut through her heart, leaving her with nothing but pain.

CHAPTER ELEVEN

I must tell her.
"You are very grave this evening."
Blinking, Jonathan tried to get his bearings, realizing that there were now three gentlemen looking at him expectantly.

"Forgive me, I was lost in thought." He tried to smile but it faltered. "Where were we?"

"We were discussing the matter of Lady Trithean and her husband," one of the other gentlemen said. "If she has shamed him, he has every right to divorce her but, for whatever reason, he has chosen not to do so. Perhaps he cannot afford the cost, or perhaps he hopes to avoid scandal. If so, he is too late."

Jonathan grimaced, then shrugged.

"I am not at all certain that such things are ours to discuss," he replied, sending a mutter of frustration through the group. "Excuse me. I think I am of little benefit here this evening. I will not hinder your discussion any longer."

Walking away, glass in hand, Jonathan tried to shake off the lingering tension which lifted his shoulders and strained his back. It had been two days since the ball and since then, Miss Fullerton had very rarely been in his company. His mother had barely said a single word to him, and Jonathan could practically feel her anger radiating from her, whenever he walked into the room. Thus far, he had not given them any explanation for his behavior but that did not mean that he intended to remain silent. By his actions, the *ton* now thought that he had considered Miss Fullerton a little too presumptuous at the ball, when that had not been his intention at all. Rather, he had intended to protect her from Lord Thornley whilst, at the same time, making certain not to divulge the truth.

Perhaps he had been wrong there.

Perhaps I could tell her the truth, and then beg her to play act for a short while? His lips flattened as the idea shattered into a thousand pieces. *Although why would she do so for my sake? It is not as though the notion would bring her any joy.*

Sighing heavily, Jonathan stopped and threw back the rest of his glass of brandy. He did not know what else there was to do. In refusing to allow Miss Fullerton to dance without any other explanation as to why, he had caused her a great deal of pain and yet, even though she did not know it, he had been attempting to protect her from what could follow. He wanted to groan aloud, for no doubt she now thought all the worse of him – perhaps even more so than she had done on their first meeting. And yet, if he told her the truth, then Jonathan feared what would happen if Lord Thornley followed through on his threat. The rumors about himself and Lady Ensley would spread, and might even lead to a duel, should Lord Ensley decide to defend either his wife's honor or seek retribution. His reputation in

London could be ruined and that would leave him rather broken.

"Good evening, Havisham."

Jonathan was brought up short by the jolly greeting which came from none other than Lord Harrogate. His anger kicked at him hard, but Jonathan contained himself with an effort, knowing that he had to be careful, given that he was at a soiree where almost every other guest could both observe and overhear him.

"You look... fatigued." Lord Harrogate's expression changed to one of concern. "Are you unwell?"

"Did you speak to Lord Thornley about Lady Ensley?" Jonathan hissed, keeping his voice as low as he could manage. "That was a matter to be kept between us!"

Lord Harrogate paled, his compassionate smile fading fast.

"I did not mean to," he replied, speaking rather quickly. "I was in my cups, and we began to discuss who we considered to be the most beautiful of ladies at present and I could not help but mention her!"

Jonathan closed his eyes and pinched the bridge of his nose, fighting to keep control of his emotions.

"You have granted Lord Thornley a boon by which he might seek to assert control."

Seeing the puzzled frown on his friend's face, Jonathan gritted his teeth so that he would not say more. No doubt Lord Thornley would use any interference – no matter how small – to declare that the bet was ruined, and the consequences would follow thereafter.

"I am sorry, old boy. I did not think Thornley would even inform you that such a thing had happened." Lord Harrogate waved a hand, once more betraying his own lack of consideration and care about such things. "But you need not worry. I am sure his word can be trusted."

"Trusted?" Jonathan repeated, disbelievingly.

"As in, he will not speak of it to anyone else," Lord Thornley replied, dismissing Jonathan's concern in an instant. "You need not look so troubled."

Jonathan took a step closer, one finger pressing towards Lord Harrogate's chest.

"You ought not to trust that particular gentleman as well as you do, Harrogate. There is more to his character than there appears."

That was the truth of it, Jonathan realized. He himself had been a little taken aback by the threat that Lord Thornley had thrown at him, having considered the gentleman to be naught more than an ordinary, genteel fellow who posed no concern to anyone. He saw Lord Harrogate frown but turned away rather than linger. There was now such a heaviness in his heart and such a confusion in his mind that he half thought about returning home rather than lingering here. A soiree would not bring him any joy, not when he was so heavily burdened.

"Good evening, Lord Havisham."

Turning, Jonathan was not surprised to see Lady Vivian. No matter where he was, she always appeared to be able to seek him out.

"Good evening, Lady Vivian. And where are your friends this evening?"

She laughed and settled one hand on his arm for a few moments, rendering Jonathan quite uncomfortable.

"They are not here at present, Lord Havisham, and I took it as an excellent opportunity to come to speak with you alone for a short time."

Jonathan allowed a heavy frown to weight itself across his brow.

"I should not like to encourage any gossip, Lady Vivian."

Again, she laughed.

"You are most considerate, but my mother is only a few steps away and, I am sure, will be watching me quite closely."

It took Jonathan a few seconds to find the lady, only for his stomach to drop as he realized she was paying no attention to Lady Vivian whatsoever of which, no doubt, the lady herself was fully aware, despite her reassurances to the contrary. Jonathan was becoming a little concerned that Lady Vivian had formed a strong connection with him whilst, for his part, he had no eagerness to develop their acquaintance further. Quite what he was to do to disabuse her of the notion that he might be interested, Jonathan had very little idea, for she certainly appeared most persistent.

"Alas, I fear I must excuse myself and go in search of my mother, as I have promised to be a little more by her side this evening." It was a fabrication, of course, but Jonathan was struggling to come up with a way to remove himself from the lady. "I fear I would not be considered much of a gentleman if I remained here rather than doing my duty to my mother."

Lady Vivian laughed and did not seem a bit put out.

"But of course." Before he could respond, she slipped her hand through his arm, coming to stand beside him. "I should be glad to greet Lady Havisham."

Jonathan's sigh was not held back but again, Lady Vivian did not appear to notice.

"But what of your mother? She will be concerned about

your absence and again, Lady Vivian, I do not wish to make any bad impressions."

"You are *very* kind to be so concerned, but my mother will have no hesitation in permitting me to go," came the confident reply. "This is only a small gathering, and I will soon be found." Her bright eyes looked up at him and Jonathan groaned inwardly. She was determined to stick with him, and he could do nothing, it seemed, to discourage her. Without having any other choice, Jonathan walked through the room in search of his mother who, no doubt, would be quite surprised to see him come to interrupt her conversation. Perhaps she would understand, although Jonathan did not think she would have any inclination to be of assistance to him, given just how frustrated and upset she was at present. "I see that Miss Fullerton has come to know her place." Jonathan's steps led them to the drawing-room door and out into the hallway which, much to his relief, was lined with various guests. The drawing room and music room were open to the guests this evening and Lady Havisham had to be in one of them! "I heard that you gave her something of a set down."

A fire lit itself in Jonathan's heart and he spoke with more fierceness than he had intended to let show.

"Miss Fullerton does not need to know her place, Lady Vivian. She is already very well aware of it and behaves with all decorum."

A snort of disbelief came from the lady, sending such an astonishment over Jonathan that, for a moment, the fire of anger in his heart dissipated.

"You need not defend your mother's companion to me! I am well aware of what was said for, whilst you may not have been aware of it, I was standing nearby when you instructed her to remain by your mother's side rather than out on the dance floor." Tutting, Lady Vivian made her opinion of Miss Fullerton known, and the spike of anger began to burrow into Jonathan's heart once more. "Your mother was most considerate to allow her such a thing as dancing, but it is right that she should not do so any longer. Not when she is a companion."

Jonathan shook his head.

"There is nothing wrong with Miss Fullerton's actions, I assure you. I spoke only to Lord Thornley."

"A gentleman of the highest regard, of course!" Lady Vivian exclaimed. "It is only right that you should not wish for him to demean himself by standing up with Miss Fullerton. The *ton* are already aware that he has shown more interest in her than would be expected."

"Miss Fullerton is able to make a match, however," Jonathan replied sharply, aware that he was coming to the lady's defense but having no qualms about doing so. "If Lord Thornley should choose –"

"I should hope that you, who are his friend, would discourage him from such a path!" Lady Vivian exclaimed, as though Jonathan was a very poor friend indeed if he did *not* do such a thing. "Good gracious, could you imagine a gentleman of quality betrothing themselves to a mere companion? That would be most embarrassing."

Jonathan blinked rapidly and gritted his teeth in an attempt to keep back the sharp, angry retort that he wanted to give to Lady Vivian. Yet, despite his best efforts, he could not hold himself back completely. Miss Fullerton did not deserve such shame and, whilst he himself had caused her pain – albeit unintentionally by attempting to do the right thing – he had every urge to protect her.

"Miss Fullerton is a genteel, quiet young lady whose circumstances have forced her into her present situation. I do not think that makes anything less of her, Lady Vivian. It is compassion and understanding which we ought to grant her and, for my part, I believe her to be quite a suitable young lady for any gentleman to consider."

Lady Vivian stopped walking just as they came to the door of the library. Turning, she looked up into his face with wide eyes, a dot of red coming into each cheek. Jonathan said nothing more but maintained his severe expression, looking back at her with steadiness and determination. He could not allow Lady Vivian to speak so cruelly of Miss Fullerton, not when she did not deserve such humiliation and cruelty.

"You surprise me, Lord Havisham." Lady Vivian's voice was soft although her lips were flat, her eyes sharp. "I would never have expected you to speak so."

"I speak as I see."

"And you see Miss Fullerton to be a genteel young lady who is worthy of making a match with any gentleman of the *ton* who might choose her?"

Lady Vivian tilted her head, but Jonathan was ready with his answer.

"Of course I do."

"Which may well include you?"

Jonathan opened his mouth to answer, ready with a confident reply, only for his heart to twist furiously in his chest and leave him a little powerless. Stammering somewhat, he cleared his throat gruffly but saw Lady Vivian's curled lip. She already had her answer.

"I think, Lady Vivian, that any gentleman who might *choose* Miss Fullerton should be considered beyond reproach. Miss Fullerton will bring him a good deal of happiness and joy, I am sure, and I am not inclined towards mockery nor considering her lower than I."

Lady Vivian's eyes narrowed.

"It appears as though you would be willing to consider Miss Fullerton over any other, Lord Havisham."

"That is a ridiculous statement," Jonathan replied, firmly. "I have no particular considerations at present." He looked back steadily into Lady Vivian's eyes and saw her eyes round suddenly, as if she had only just become aware of what he meant. A small, satisfied smile tugged at the corners of his mouth, but he did not say anything more, relieved now that Lady Vivian understood what he had been trying to convey for some time now.

"I see." Lady Vivian's hand slowly crept away from his arm before she clasped both hands tightly in front of her. "You have no intentions towards any young lady at present?"

"None." Jonathan lifted his chin a notch, making himself as clear as he could. "I am, at present, a very contented bachelor, Lady Vivian."

Her eyes shifted away from his face for a few moments and Jonathan feared that she might break down in tears. However, that fear was soon removed for when Lady Vivian looked back at him, her eyes were clear, although there was a tightness about her lips which was unmistakable.

"I am not certain that I believe you, Lord Havisham."

A little surprised, Jonathan let out a small chuckle.

"I do not think that it matters whether or not you do so, Lady Vivian."

She did not seem to hear him, stepping closer and speaking in hushed tones.

"I believe that Miss Fullerton has more of a hold on you than you wish to admit. I am convinced that you feel something significant for her, given how much you have sought to defend her."

"You are being ridiculous."

Her smile was closer to a sneer.

"I do not believe so. But have no doubt, Lord Havisham, you are making a foolish mistake to pursue such a lady when there is far better before you." Jonathan said nothing, not wanting to express to Lady Vivian the truth of his thoughts for fear that would make her all the more upset. To his mind, when considering Lady Vivian and Miss Fullerton, there was no comparison. The latter was far more than the former, both in terms of character and indeed, as regarded his own considerations of them both. "You will see the truth very soon, I am determined." Lady Vivian surprised him by stepping closer still, her breath brushing across his face, her hand reaching up to press lightly against his heart as though she were determined to force her way into his affections. "You must only pray that it is not too late."

Turning on her heel, Lady Vivian departed, stepping into the music room, and leaving him to stand alone. Jonathan let out a long sigh, allowing it to roll forward and out from his chest, taking away a good deal of tension with it. He had, at least, made himself quite clear with Lady Vivian and could only pray that she now turned her attentions elsewhere. Quite what she had meant by her last few words he did not know, but Jonathan quickly threw any concern aside. If she stayed far from him, then he would have naught to concern himself with.

"Good evening, Lord Havisham."

A soft voice caught his ears and he half-turned, just as Miss Fullerton walked directly past him. Her hands were clasped in front of her, her head held high, and she did not so much as glance at him as she made her way to the music room.

"Miss Fullerton, I –"

Just how much did she see?

Jonathan closed his eyes as Miss Fullerton continued walking, making no sign of even considering stopping or returning to his company to listen to what he had to say. Instead, she went directly into the music room and allowed the door to swing closed behind her, leaving him standing, his words unfinished on his lips.

Dropping his head, Jonathan raked one hand through his hair, groaning aloud. Miss Fullerton had, certainly, seen or heard something, but what it was, he could not be sure. The accusations that Lady Vivian had flung at him about caring for Miss Fullerton rang in his ears and Jonathan did not immediately throw them aside. Instead, he allowed them to linger, let them push their way into his heart so that he might consider all that lay there. Yes, he *did* want to protect Miss Fullerton. Yes, he *was* drawn to her in a way that he could not explain, for even their waltz together had not left his mind in some days. And yes, he did think her better than any other young lady of his acquaintance, even though she was lower in standing than many of them.

What did such feelings and considerations mean? Was Lady Vivian correct when she stated that he felt something significant for the lady? And if he did, then what was he meant to do next?

CHAPTER TWELVE

Try as she might, Deborah could not remove the memory of Lady Vivian brushing her hand lightly across Lord Havisham's chest. Nor could she push away the words that she had overheard, her heart sinking low in her chest every time she considered them. Lady Vivian clearly had every intention of declaring her feelings in full to Lord Havisham and he, in turn, would be unable to turn away from them, Deborah was quite sure. She fully expected that a courtship, if not a betrothal, would be announced soon and, whilst she wanted very much to be glad for Lord Havisham, there came such a strange, unrelenting pain in her heart at the thought. It was a pain so strong that Deborah felt as though she could never escape it.

"You are tired, my dear."

Deborah smiled as Lady Havisham came to sit down opposite her at the breakfast table. She had managed to arrive before the lady this morning, although it was a good deal later than they usually broke their fast. Last evening had been an enjoyable, but very late, affair and even now, Deborah had to admit that she was fatigued.

"I am quite well."

"My son has not appeared as yet?"

Deborah's smile flew from her lips.

"Not as yet, Lady Havisham."

The lady frowned, grimacing as she did so.

"He is avoiding my company – *our* company, I am sure of it." Choosing not to give air to her thoughts – which were that she did not mind the lack of Lord Havisham's company – Deborah merely gave Lady Havisham a soft smile and then turned to her attention to buttering her toast. "That Lady Vivian was with him again last evening."

Deborah nodded, ignoring the kick of pain which came with the mention of the lady's name.

"Indeed, I believe so. Lord Havisham must be very inclined to her company."

Lady Havisham snorted.

"Well, if he is, then he has not informed me of it. Although I will say that I know he has not been going to call upon her as yet." She poured her own tea and then stirred it carefully. "Perhaps that will come in time."

Deborah's lips bunched, but she remained silent. Lady Vivian might well be a suitable match for Lord Havisham in terms of her wealth and social standing, but from what Deborah had overheard and seen of Lady Vivian's character, she thought her entirely unmatched with Lord Havisham. It was a little surprising to her that, even though Lord Havisham had treated her in such a dreadful manner at the last ball, she still found herself thinking well of him on the whole.

A small sigh escaped her lips, noticed by Lady Havisham. As yet, Lord Havisham had not explained his reasons for demanding that she no longer step out with any other gentleman that evening. Whenever she thought of it,

Deborah's chest grew tight and her eyes hot, just as they did at this very moment. Trying to steady herself, Deborah closed her eyes quickly and took in a long, calming breath in what she hoped was a surreptitious manner.

They had not spoken of it since that evening and she, for her part, struggled to even look at Lord Havisham with any sort of steadiness. She was waiting for him to bring up the subject in conversation, waiting for him to say something – anything – about why he had forbidden her from dancing, but as yet, he had not said a word. Confusion, upset and shame all tied themselves together within her but still, within her core there lay a small, flickering hope that Lord Havisham had done such a thing for a good and wholesome reason. She had enough experience of his renewed character to allow such a hope to continue burning, even though it was beginning to weaken with every day that passed. Another sigh left her lips as she opened her eyes, reaching to stir her tea. Lord Havisham would not leave her thoughts and Deborah, for her part, had no desire to remove him from her mind as yet.

Her shoulders dropped as the memory of his fingers brushing across her cheek threw itself at her heart. There had been a tenderness in that moment which had both frightened and exhilarated her and that, she was sure, had led to her enviousness over Lord Havisham dancing with Lady Vivian. In the depths of her heart, Deborah confessed quietly to herself that she wanted Lord Havisham to look at her as though she were the only lady worthy of his attention – even though such a thing could never be.

"You are quiet this morning."

Her eyes flew up to meet Lady Havisham's.

"My apologies. I –"

"You do not need to apologize." Lady Havisham interrupted her with a gentle smile. "There is something on your mind, I think, and I have no doubt that you are thinking of my son."

A rush of heat flew up into Deborah's cheeks and she cleared her throat, not quite certain what it was that she was meant to say to such a thing. Had Lady Havisham known her thoughts? Had there been something in her expression that told her of it?

"I do hope he will give you an explanation soon."

Deborah tried to smile, picking up her teacup as though the warm drink would cover up the pink in her cheeks.

"He is not required to."

"He will have no other choice but to give me an explanation," Lady Havisham stated, firmly. "I shall not rest until I understand it!"

"It may very well be that I have overstepped my place," Deborah answered, as Lady Havisham's frown grew. "He might have thought my dance card full enough."

Lady Havisham shook her head.

"That is not consistent with what he stated. Regardless, my dear, I will have the truth from him. You need not worry about the ball this evening. I am sure that Lord Thornley will be *eager* to dance with you since he was already so badly denied."

Deborah nodded, but her smile did not spread across her face. Lord Thornley did not capture her thoughts as Lord Havisham did. Even though he treated her with more consideration and certainly seemed eager for her company, she did not find her heart at all engaged with him.

But does such a thing matter, if I am to find a suitable husband? Her mouth pulled downwards. *One's heart does not have to hold any affection for one's husband, I suppose. Not when my need for a husband is so pressing.*

"Do not be downhearted, my dear." Lady Havisham smiled, clearly eager to reassure her. "At the ball this evening, everything will be just as it ought – and who knows? By the end of the night, you might find yourself with more than Lord Thornley eager for your company!"

Deborah tried to smile, but it did not come easily. She was not looking forward to the ball nor to Lord Thornley's company. With everything that had taken place, and everything that she now felt, she was unsure and unsteady as if walking on uneven ground and with no certain sense of what was to come.

~

"Ah, Miss Fullerton."

Deborah looked up, a little surprised to see Lady Vivian walking towards her. The ball had been in full swing for a little over an hour and she and Lady Havisham had only arrived a few minutes ago. Lady Havisham was in deep discussion with a friend and Deborah had chosen to stand back quietly so that she would not be an interruption.

"You and I are not properly introduced, but I do not think that such a thing matters." Lady Vivian's smile curved but there was no warmth in her eyes. Her gaze flicked up and down Deborah's form and Deborah herself blushed at her scrutiny, all too aware of her simple gown compared to Lady Vivian's ornate one. "I expect you are wondering why I have deigned to come to converse with you."

The sneer in Lady Vivian's voice made Deborah's stomach tighten. She had no need to stand and converse with the lady, regardless of whether or not Lady Vivian wished to do so. To be treated with such disdain was not something she had tolerated from Lord Havisham, and she certainly would not be willing to tolerate it now.

"If you will excuse me, I am waiting for Lady Havisham to finish her conversation."

Dropping into a small curtsey, she flicked Lady Vivian a half-smile before physically turning away from her. The sneer on Lady Vivian's face dropped in an instant, replaced with a harsh glare as she tightened her jaw, but Deborah did not react. Instead, she kept her head turned away and looked directly towards Lady Havisham rather than giving any attention to Lady Vivian.

A cold hand grasped her arm, making Deborah catch her breath. Lady Vivian yanked her back towards her, her eyes shards of glass, cutting into Deborah.

"You will not trifle with me, Miss Fullerton!" Lady Vivian hissed, her face close to Deborah's. "You may have been given additional freedoms, courtesy of Lady Havisham's much too generous nature, but you will not find me relenting and treating you as though you are an equal."

Deborah's heart clattered against her chest, but she grasped hold of her small, flailing courage and pulled it to the surface.

"In that case, I find it exceedingly strange indeed that you should come to speak to me, Lady Vivian, given that I am so very far below you."

Lady Vivian drew back and for a moment, Deborah feared that she would strike her. Her face a mottled red, Lady Vivian let out a hiss of breath. Heat ran across Deborah's cheek.

"You are attempting to garner Lord Havisham's affections."

Deborah's eyes widened.

"Indeed, I am not."

"I am well aware of your intentions." Lady Vivian kept her voice low, but anger threaded through every word. "You reside in his house and think that you can pull him towards you simply by your presence there, but I will not allow you to do such a thing. He is meant for me. We intend to wed by the end of the Season, and you will *not* force yourself in between us!"

It was as if Lady Vivian had struck her, for all the air left Deborah's lungs, forcing her to bend forward as she fought to catch her breath. Lady Vivian drew herself up to her full height whilst Deborah closed her eyes, trying hard to draw in as much air as she could.

Wed?

Lord Havisham was then secretly betrothed to Lady Vivian, it seemed. Neither Lady Havisham nor herself knew of such a thing and the pain which shot through her at the thought seemed to bend every bone in her body. In that one, startling moment, Deborah realized the truth.

She cared for Lord Havisham.

Her eyes remained closed as Lady Vivian began to chuckle, evidently believing that Deborah's reaction came from a realization of guilt or being set back in her place. Deborah could not form words, and remained with her head bowed, her hands balling into fists as she bit down hard on her lip. She would say nothing more to Lady Vivian. Not now. Not when it was clear that Lord Havisham had already attached his affections to the lady. She could not risk doing so.

"I trust that I will not see you standing up to dance with Lord Havisham again."

Lady Vivian was gone in a whirl of skirts, leaving Deborah trying to regain some sort of composure. Her throat constricted, and stars danced in front of her eyes as she blinked. Lady Havisham laughed as she continued her conversation with her friend, seemingly entirely unaware of Deborah's struggle.

It all made sense to her now. Lord Havisham had prevented her from dancing any further at that ball at Lady Vivian's behest. She thought him too kind, too generous and thus had insisted that he prevent her from standing up again – and now Lady Vivian had come to speak to her directly so that she made herself absolutely clear. Deborah had never considered Lord Havisham to be a gentleman so easily bent to another's will, but if he cared for Lady Vivian, then it seemed right that he would do as she asked. How much she herself must have angered Lady Vivian by dancing with Lord Havisham! And how much pain she now felt knowing that such a thing would never take place again.

Her stomach twisted and she closed her eyes tight. The realization that she had come to care for Lord Havisham brought her nothing but pain. It was too late. It was much too late. He was now to be wed to Lady Vivian and there was nothing that she could do. Lord Thornley was her only hope for a suitable husband and even then, Deborah had no doubt that she would continually yearn and think of another.

"And are you to dance this evening, Miss Fullerton?"

Deborah swallowed at the tightness in her throat, lifting her head to see none other than Lord Thornley before her.

"I – I do not know, Lord Thornley. Lord Havisham has said nothing to me about this evening and–"

"But of *course,* she is dancing." Lady Havisham's bright voice was filled with encouragement as she came towards them both. "Lord Havisham was a little out of sorts at the last ball and spoke without consideration."

Shaking her head, Deborah put one hand on Lady

Havisham's arm, turning to her and speaking in a low voice. After the interaction she had endured with Lady Vivian, she could not continue without hearing from Lord Havisham first.

"I should prefer to speak to Lord Havisham before accepting," she murmured, as Lady Havisham frowned. "Please, I cannot displease him again."

Lady Havisham turned back to Lord Thornley, reaching across to pat Deborah's hand.

"Why do you not choose your dances, Lord Thornley, and in the interim, Miss Fullerton will make certain that my son has no complaint. As I have said, I am sure that there will be no difficulty, but the dear girl is quite insistent that she has his agreement."

"You have an excellent character, Miss Fullerton," Lord Thornley grinned, as Deborah handed him her dance card, albeit with some reluctance. "I am certain that Lord Havisham will have no cause to disagree."

Lady Havisham turned, then gestured to Deborah.

"He is standing just there, Miss Fullerton. Why do you not speak to him now?"

Deborah nodded and then stepped away from them both. Her stomach was in knots, her hands tying tight to each other as she walked towards him. Lord Havisham was laughing at something someone else had said and as she approached, Deborah dropped her head, afraid now of interrupting him.

"Indeed, I find that most invigorating!" Lord Havisham agreed, as Deborah drew near, but then stopped, standing a little away from him. "Ah, excuse me, old boy. I must just speak to Miss Fullerton." His hand settled on Deborah's arm, and she jumped, his touch startling her.

"My Lord, I...." Deborah fought to find the right words

to say. "I beg your pardon for interrupting you, but I must know whether or not I have your permission to dance."

Lord Havisham cleared his throat gruffly and Deborah dared a glance at him. His green eyes had darkened, and his chin was jutting forward gently. It seemed that she was not to have his permission to dance.

"I am not to be referred to as, 'my Lord', Miss Fullerton. And I understand now that I have created a problem where there ought not to be any. However, the situation is more complicated than it appears."

Deborah nodded, already aware of what it was that he meant.

"I understand, Lord Havisham. It was, perhaps, a mistake for me to dance with you. I apologize."

There was a breath of silence and then he caught her hand, tugging her a little closer to him. Deborah's eyes flew to his, her heart suddenly slamming hard against her chest.

"No, Miss Fullerton, there was nothing wrong in our dancing." His voice was low but fervent as if he was begging her to believe him. "I have not said anything of the sort and certainly do not think that there was any sort of concern in that regard. Did you not enjoy our dance together?"

Deborah pressed her lips together gently, finding it hard to answer such a simple question.

"I did."

"And you do not wish to dance with me again?" A gentleness came into his voice that sent warmth flooding over her, heat warming her cheeks. What was she to say? Yes, she very much *did* want to dance with him again, to feel his arms around her, to have him hold her close. Lowering her eyes, she spread her hands, unable to give him a verbal answer. "I am embarrassing you now, am I not?" Much to her astonishment, his thumb began to brush the back of her hand, sending sparks shooting up her arm as her breath hitched. "I have not done well to explain all of this to you, Miss Fullerton. I have been embarrassed and frustrated and, quite frankly, a little selfish. *Very* selfish, in fact. I ought not to have been so but alas, I shall confess that it has held me back."

"Then..." Deborah looked up at him again, holding his gaze this time. "Do you permit me to dance?"

"Is it with Lord Thornley?"

Deborah nodded.

"He has asked me, yes."

"And do you wish to?"

This time, her answer did not come as quickly as the other. Instead, she bit her lip, spreading one hand as though to express that she had very little choice.

"If Lord Thornley is interested in my company, it would be unwise to refuse him."

Lord Havisham pressed her hand, shook his head, and then released her.

"I will not prevent you, Miss Fullerton. But you and I must speak. We should have done so before now, but I will satisfy myself that we will do so tomorrow, at your earliest convenience."

She nodded, having no knowledge at all as to what he wished to explain to her but glad that shortly, she was to have a full explanation of why he had told her not to dance any longer during that previous ball.

"Promise me you will not give too much time and attention to Lord Thornley." His eyes searched hers and Deborah nodded her agreement, seeing the small, satisfied smile which spread light up into his eyes. "And promise me that you will allow me to dance with you also."

She nodded again, aware of the fire spreading through

her veins. Lord Havisham was behaving in the most extraordinary way, and it was more than she had ever expected to hear from him.

But what of Lady Vivian?

"I am not certain that such a thing would sit well with...." Deborah broke off without completing her sentence, having no eagerness to inform Lord Havisham of her conversation with Lady Vivian. "If you are certain that it will bring no upset then, of course."

"It shall bring only great delight and joy, I assure you."

Deborah blinked in surprise but did not make any further comment. Silently, she began to question what Lady Vivian had said to her, wondering if the assumptions she had made were not, perhaps, correct. Lord Havisham seemed eager to dance with her, which went entirely against what Lady Vivian had stated.

"You will save me the country dance, mayhap?"

She nodded.

"But of course. Thank you."

Lord Havisham's smile brought a lightness to Deborah's spirits which she had not experienced in some days and, as she turned away from him, she found a small, bright smile pulling at her lips. Yes, there was still a great deal of confusion, and certainly, she was not at all sure of what Lady Vivian had meant by coming to speak to her as she had, but that was something she could think of later, perhaps after Lord Havisham's conversation with her tomorrow.

She was eager for things to finally be made clear.

CHAPTER THIRTEEN

"Miss Fullerton. Lord Havisham has left you this note."

Deborah turned in her chair as Lady Havisham looked on in surprise. The butler was holding out a small note towards her and Deborah took it at once, a little taken aback.

"A note from my son to Miss Fullerton?"

"Yes, my Lady."

The butler nodded and, after enquiring as to whether or not there was anything else required of him, withdrew. Deborah opened the note quickly, her eyes scanning the short few lines.

"We were to meet this morning to discuss what took place at the ball – as regards Lord Havisham being unwilling to permit me to dance," she murmured, surprised how disappointed she felt at the fact that such a thing would now not take place. "He has been called into town to deal with an urgent business matter and asks that we meet tomorrow instead."

"I see." Lady Havisham smiled, although there was a

question in her eyes which Deborah prayed she would not ask aloud. "Although my son did permit you to dance last evening, which I was glad of. Did you enjoy the evening? Lord Thornley *and* Lord Harrogate were both very attentive, although I am sure that you preferred the company of one over the other."

Deborah gave her a small smile.

"Lord Harrogate is not a gentleman I would permit to pursue me, given all that Lord Havisham has told me of him," she agreed. "Lord Thornley is most attentive also, however, as you have said."

"And do you think well of him?"

Chewing over her answer, Deborah took a few moments to respond.

"I think Lord Thornley an engaging gentleman, and would accept his court, should he offer it."

A dull clang sounded in her heart as though she were sealing her fate somehow, but Deborah did her best to ignore it. If Lord Havisham was either betrothed or considering betrothal to Lady Vivian – which was quite right and proper and to be expected – then she could not allow her feelings for him to hold her back from her own future.

"Good." Lady Havisham tapped the table with one finger. "Then I think we shall make our way into town and purchase you a gown for the ball this evening. Something a little finer."

Deborah's eyes opened wide.

"Lady Havisham, there is no need! I am truly grateful for all that you have given me thus far and do not require anything more."

"Nonsense!" Lady Havisham beamed as she rose from the table. "You deserve a great deal more, my dear. We must make sure that particular gentlemen realize the depths of your beauty so that they will make up their minds to act rather than simply to stand and admire you."

A small knot of fear tightened in Deborah's stomach.

"And you do not think that my father will hear of any of this?"

"No, I do not." Lady Havisham's confidence assuaged Deborah's fears. "You know that he cares nothing for London or the *ton,* and will push away even the smallest mention of it! Besides which, who would tell him of your presence here?"

That was a question which Deborah could not answer and, with her spirits lifted and her fears pushed away, there was nothing for her to do but rise and follow Lady Havisham.

~

"Good evening, Miss Fullerton."

Deborah smiled, her blush a little increased even though she did not think much of the gentleman. His admiration of her was more than obvious in the widening of his eyes and the way he cleared the surprise from his throat.

"Good evening, Lord Harrogate."

"You are dancing this evening, I hope?"

"But of course." It was as though she were not a companion at all, as though this evening, she was naught but a lady in her own right rather than a paid worker. The gown she wore had gold and silver threads running through it, which Deborah knew caught the light whenever she moved. Lace adorned the sleeves, the neck, and the hem, and new soft slippers encased her feet. It had taken Lady Havisham a good deal of effort to convince Deborah to accept the gown, but in the end, she had succeeded. Now, standing here in the ballroom, Deborah was glad that she had chosen to accept. Regardless of what came from this evening, she would not forget this night.

"Thank you, Lord Harrogate."

"I look forward to our dances together, Miss Fullerton."

She smiled again, but watched him depart with sharp eyes. Lord Harrogate was not a gentleman whom she was at all inclined towards, not now after Lord Havisham had told her the truth of his motivations. And yet she appreciated his willingness to stand up with her. Her gaze strayed across the room until they caught and held onto another, her breath hitching as she did so.

Lord Havisham was looking at her as though he had never seen her before. His gaze was fixed and staring, his eyes rounded and his jaw slack. Someone was speaking to him, but he was not responding to them in any way, as if he had quite forgotten that he was in the middle of a conversation.

Her stomach flipped over as he began to walk towards her, his expression never changing. Her heart began to beat hard against her chest, making her breathless with anticipation. She did not know what she expected from him, but even just to have him near would bring her a great deal of happiness.

"Miss Fullerton." Lord Havisham's voice was low and a little husky. "Good evening."

She dropped into a curtsey.

"Good evening, Lord Havisham. I received your note earlier today. I thank you for your consideration."

He blinked at her owlishly.

"Note?"

"About our conversation which was to take place."

Nodding, he closed his eyes as if closing out the sight of her would help him gain enough clarity to respond.

"Yes, of course."

"Miss Fullerton is dancing this evening." Lady Havisham put one hand on Deborah's shoulder, pushing her forward just a fraction. "It would be good if you might consider standing up with her also."

"Also?" Lord Havisham held out one hand and Deborah quickly placed her dance card into it, seeing him frown. "Lord Harrogate has already come forward, I see. I shall not permit you to have only *his* company, however." He quickly wrote his name down and then returned the card to Deborah. "Another waltz, Miss Fullerton, since our last one was so very enjoyable."

His fingers brushed hers as he returned her dance card and Deborah pulled her hand back a little too quickly as fire shot up through her fingers. Lord Havisham's smile was a little crooked as he looked back at her, as if he had felt the very same.

"Might I say, Miss Fullerton, that you look remarkably beautiful this evening."

Deborah did not know how to respond, looking up into his eyes and finding herself so overcome by all that she felt and his nearness to her, that speaking even a single word seemed impossible.

"I am certain that you will garner a great deal of attention this evening, but I must claim the waltz for myself." Reaching out, he took her hand and, much to Deborah's astonishment, bent over it, his lips brushing the back of her hand. Nothing more was said between them, but as he released her hand and then turned away, Deborah was all too aware of the heat which had swirled between them.

She did not understand it. Her eyes lingered on him as

he moved away, no longer hearing anything of the ball around her. If Lady Vivian was as dear to him as the lady herself had stated, then why had he done such a thing as kissing the back of her hand? Such an action was an intimate, meaningful gesture and Deborah did not know what to make of it.

Her gaze snagged on a pair of sharp eyes flashing back at her. Blinking, she quickly realized that it was none other than Lady Vivian who, from the way her lip curled, was clearly furious with what she had witnessed. Her stomach rolled, but Deborah did not drop her head or allow herself to be cowed. She was here this evening in her own right and if Lord Havisham wished to dance with her, then Deborah was not about to refuse him. Lady Vivian narrowed her eyes, but after some moments, tossed her head and turned sharply, cutting off their connection.

Deborah let out a long, slow breath. Whatever was between Lord Havisham and Lady Vivian was not anything to do with her, and if Lady Vivian was displeased, then she would have to discuss it with Lord Havisham rather than herself. With a small lift of her chin, Deborah turned back towards Lady Havisham, ready to greet whoever came to speak to her next.

~

"OH, Miss Fullerton, I am so very glad that I have found you!"

Deborah blinked in surprise.

"Miss Newfield. You are a little out of breath, are you quite well?"

"I have been a fool!" Miss Newfield shook her head, her red curls flying. "I told you that Lady Vivian and Lord

Havisham were to wed very soon but it seems that the connection between them has been entirely fabricated! Lady Vivian is very angry this evening about something which involves Lord Havisham, but when I stated that she had nothing to worry about since they were betrothed, the truth came out!"

Her world began to narrow, and Deborah stared into Miss Newfield's eyes. Remembering what she had heard from Lady Vivian some time ago about gaining a gentleman's attention one way or the other, Deborah felt her heart squeeze with both fright and pain.

"She is not betrothed?" she whispered, as Miss Newfield nodded fervently. "There is naught between them?"

"Only what Lady Vivian has created," Miss Newfield returned, her eyes still wide. "I am truly sorry, Miss Fullerton. I did not mean to deceive you."

Deborah reached out and grasped her hand.

"And you did not. That was not a deliberate act, I hold nothing against you."

Miss Newfield's expression was pinched.

"I came to beg of you to speak to Lord Havisham, Miss Fullerton. Lady Vivian was so angry that she told me she has every intention of making certain that Lord Havisham has no other choice but to claim her as his bride. I could not speak to him myself, of course, for fear of being found out by Lady Vivian – you will think me a coward, Miss Fullerton, but the lady could easily make things very difficult for me – but I come to you in the hope that you will be able to do so."

Deborah nodded fervently, looking around for Lady Havisham but seeing her a short distance away, speaking fervently to two others.

"But of course. I – I will go in search of him at once."

It was not proper for her to do so, given that she ought to stay by Lady Havisham's side, but the urgency which flooded her demanded that she act.

"Thank you, Miss Fullerton."

Deborah pressed Miss Newfield's hand and then hurried away, walking through the ballroom and in between the guests. Her eyes roved over each and every face, trying to discover him, but he was not to be found.

The room was very large indeed and there were a huge number of guests, rendering Deborah rather hopeless that she would ever be able to discover him. Her waltz was not for some time yet and Lord Havisham might be anywhere in amongst the crowd of the ballroom – if not in the card room or wandering in the gardens! A little panicked, Deborah pressed one hand to her stomach, fighting to keep hold of her composure. In her mind's eye, Deborah saw Lady Vivian reaching for Lord Havisham, grasping for him in as wanton a manner as she could display, knowing that, in doing so, the *ton* would think there was much affection between Lord Havisham and Lady Vivian, and would expect marriage thereafter.

I must stop this. A knife twisted in her gut as the vision played out again. *For his sake, I must find him.*

Her breath caught as she saw Lady Vivian, her head bent low towards that of another young lady. Miss Newfield stood by her, her face still rather pale and her lips pinched in clear distress. Deborah, her heart hammering, watched as Lady Vivian turned on her heel, her delicate curls swinging gently as she walked purposefully in one direction. Having no other recourse, Deborah followed her.

Lady Vivian walked beside her friend, arm in arm and clearly without a single thought about the fact that she was, at present, unchaperoned by her mother. Deborah assumed that they would remain in the ballroom, only to come to a hesitant stop as both ladies walked out into the hallway.

She glanced over her shoulder. Had she been in any other gown then she might very well have been ignored but, given that she was dressed in finery, her walking alone would be noticed by someone, surely? Her eyes closed but she thought only of Lord Havisham. Risking her reputation would be worth it, if she were to save him from scandal and, thereafter, a lifetime of misery. Taking a deep breath, Deborah set her shoulders, lifted her chin, and walked directly out after Lady Vivian, her footsteps muffled on the soft carpet. It did not take her long to catch Lady Vivian and Lady Catherine, for they were walking slowly now and with their heads bent close together. Keeping as far back as she could, Deborah waited quietly in the shadows, seeing them stop altogether. Then, with a final nod and press of the hands, Lady Vivian slipped away whilst Lady Catherine turned to the left, making her way along the hallway. Deborah hurried forward, turning her head but Lady Vivian was already gone.

What am I to do?

Deborah swallowed hard, looking from one side to the other. She had no knowledge of where Lady Vivian might be, but Lady Catherine it seemed did was making her way to the card room. Hurrying forward, Deborah ensconced herself in a small alcove, peering around it carefully. She could still make out Lady Catherine thanks to the many candles which burned to light the hallway whilst she remained hidden in shadow.

He must be in there. They must have known that he went to the card room.

Silently, Deborah watched from the corner of the

hallway as Lady Catherine spoke to the footman near the card room, her urgent tones floating down towards her. Whatever she was saying, the footman nodded and then disappeared inside – only for Lady Catherine to flee down the hallway. Deborah pulled back sharply, frightened that she would be seen, but Lady Catherine swept by without a backward glance. Deborah followed her with her eyes, seeing her disappear along the hallway in the opposite direction and making no attempt to return to the ballroom. Whatever it was Lady Vivian had planned, Deborah knew it was not good.

"An urgent matter, did you say?" Lord Havisham's voice swept down the hallway and Deborah closed her eyes, staying exactly where she was for fear that she would be seen by one or more gentlemen who might then wonder what she was doing hiding herself in such a place. "Where is the lady?"

"I suspect she returned to your mother, my Lord." The footman cleared his throat. "The parlor is only a little way further past the ballroom. Shall I accompany you?"

Deborah did not hear his reply but the sound of only one set of footsteps caught her ears and she let out a slow breath. Turning, she peered around the edge of the alcove again, just as Lord Havisham drew near. Without having any thought as to what she was doing, Deborah reached out and grasped his arm, tugging him quickly towards her.

"Lord Havisham!"

Her whisper and her grasp startled him for he let out a small exclamation and, off balance, practically fell against her. The wind was knocked from her lungs but the relief which poured into her whole being was overwhelming and she sagged against him. Regardless of what happened now, regardless of who had noticed her walking from the ballroom without Lady Havisham, at least Lord Havisham was safe.

"Miss Fullerton?"

Lord Havisham stared down at her in the gloom and Deborah nodded, barely able to lift her head.

"Are you all right?"

His hands were on her arms, stroking down towards her hands, his fingers brushing hers before catching them completely.

"I am well," she breathed, her chest still aching but her relief unbounded. "Lord Havisham, I must –"

Her words were cut off as, in that one, beautiful moment, his head lowered, and his mouth caught hers. The heat of his kiss burned her, rendering her senseless. All thoughts flew from her head, all concern fled from her heart as she lost herself completely in Lord Havisham's kiss.

CHAPTER FOURTEEN

I am kissing her.

The astonishment of what he was doing still ran through Jonathan as he tilted his head and deepened their kiss a little more. His hand freed itself from her fingers, only to reach up and cradle her cheek as she tentatively rested both hands lightly against his chest. This was so entirely unexpected and yet it felt as though he had just found something so incredibly precious that he did not want to let her go. The awareness of just how much she had come to mean to him suddenly dropped heavily into his mind, his breath hitching all the more.

He broke the kiss reluctantly, hearing the raggedness of her breathing.

"When I saw you this evening, I was certain that I had never before seen anything so beautiful," he whispered, all too aware of just how much her beauty had struck him. He had been unable to pull his eyes away, lost in the wonder of her and struggling to make sense of the great myriad of emotions that had swamped him. "I had to have the waltz with you, for it is the most intimate and I could not have you share it with any other."

Miss Fullerton closed her eyes and dragged in air, her hands still flat against his chest.

"Lord Havisham, I –" She shook her head tightly as if demanding silently that she return to her previous intentions. But then her shoulders dropped, and she smiled, opening her eyes. "I wanted very much to dance it with you, Lord Havisham."

There was a slight air of nervousness flowing from her, as though she was concerned that he would suddenly step back from her, satisfied with what had taken place and then requiring nothing more of her.

"There has been so much confusion between us, has there not?" Gently, he tipped her chin up, bending his head just to look into her eyes a little more. "I have not yet explained myself as regards Lord Thornley and the dancing and the ball – but you must know that some of it came from my own desires to be with you."

Blinking, Miss Fullerton let out a small sigh and then smiled.

"Truly?"

"I speak the truth! I am astonished at myself, but I must confess it to you."

Her smile faded.

"I am not at all of your standing."

His heart stuttered and his hand wrapped around her waist, pulling her a little closer to him.

"That is not what I meant, Miss Fullerton. When I say that I am astonished at myself, it is not because I consider you to be lesser than I, nor that I am surprised that I have come to care for someone such as you – more that I am astonished at the depth of feeling which has suddenly overwhelmed me. I did not ever think I would feel anything akin to this – and yet you, Miss Fullerton, have brought these feelings to the fore."

"Oh." Her lips curved lightly again, and he could almost feel the relief that came from her. On instinct, Jonathan dropped his head and kissed her again, albeit with a very light touch indeed. Letting out a long breath, he lifted his head and tried to think clearly. "Is – is there a reason that you are hiding here, Miss Fullerton?" Up until now, he had not even thought about why she had been hiding in an alcove and had pulled him in towards her. "I have only just realized that... and my mother?" An urgency burned in his mind, and he caught his breath. "Why did you tell the footman that my mother is unwell and needs me if you were then to hide here?"

She shook her head.

"I did not give you any such message. Your mother is quite well! She is in the ballroom and does not know of my absence." Her teeth caught her bottom lip for a moment, clearly concerned. "I came here alone, following Lady Vivian."

Confusion wrapped around him.

"Lady Vivian?"

Miss Fullerton nodded.

"There is a long and convoluted explanation required, but for the moment all that is required is to state that Lady Vivian intends to make certain that you and she become betrothed."

Shock slammed hard against him.

"Betrothed?"

"Some days ago, she came to speak to me directly, insisting that I should not stand up to dance with you again, and stating that you were soon to be betrothed to her. At the time, I believed that this was the reason for your eagerness to prevent me from dancing. I thought that it was at *her* behest, which then confused me all the more when you stated that you wished to dance with me again."

Jonathan closed his eyes.

"Good gracious. I had no knowledge of her intentions."

"Miss Newfield was of great help and informed me that there was no betrothal, only the desire for one on Lady Vivian's side. Given what I had overheard, I came at once to prevent you from being caught up in her plan. It was only by sheer luck that I saw Lady Vivian and Lady Catherine leave the ballroom! Had I been only a few minutes later, then...." She did not finish her sentence but closed her eyes tightly, giving him a small shake of her head. Letting out a long, slow breath, Jonathan let his fingers skim lightly across her cheek before pulling her tight against him. "It was Lady Catherine who gave you that message," he heard her say, her voice a little muffled. "I have no doubt that Lady Vivian is waiting for you in the parlor – and that Lady Catherine will be nearby, ready to capture whatever moment it is that she intends to create. And likely to set up a loud outcry, to bring the attention of others."

A vision of Lady Vivian wrapping her arms around his neck and holding on tightly until Lady Catherine walked in sent trails of ice running down his back.

"I have no doubt that your expectation is quite correct. Oh, Miss Fullerton, I believe that I am quite in your debt!" His hands cupped her face, his heart suddenly aching for her, even though he was standing as close to her as he could be. "And in coming in search of me, you have risked a great deal. The *ton* will notice if you and I return together."

"But I cannot stay here indefinitely!"

"No, you cannot. Therefore, Miss Fullerton, let us allow

the *ton* to watch us. Let them see us walk back into the room together with your hand on my arm. I have no hesitation in doing so, Miss Fullerton. Not after what we have shared here together." He could not see her blush in the shadows, but he was sure that her cheeks were a delicate, gentle pink. Her smile was unmistakable however and, when he turned, her hand was at his arm in an instant. "Lady Vivian shall not have me," he murmured, as they stepped out of the alcove together. "Of that, I am quite determined." As they neared the ballroom, the first strains of the waltz came towards him and, looking down at Miss Fullerton, Jonathan smiled, reached across, and patted her hand. "It seems as though we are to be able to dance the waltz, Miss Fullerton. I do hope that you are still willing to step out with me?"

Her eyes sparkled, swirling with hints of gold as she smiled her agreement up at him.

"I am, Lord Havisham."

A deep sense of contentment settled in his chest as he walked out into the ballroom with Miss Fullerton on his arm. She had saved him from Lady Vivian's intentions, and he could not have felt more gratitude. Yes, he required a little time now to consider his feelings for her and what the future now meant for them both but, for the moment, he would enjoy dancing with her once more.

"Lord Havisham."

Jonathan quickly rearranged his features from a grimace into a genial expression, not wanting Lady Vivian to have any awareness of the deep and cutting dislike that now filled him. After all, she would not know that it had been Miss Fullerton who had saved him from stumbling into her clutches, and Jonathan did not intend even to mention the matter. Bowing, he smiled as best he could, noting the paleness in Lady Vivian's cheeks and how her returning smile did nothing to brighten her eyes.

"We are to dance, I believe."

"Oh." He had quite forgotten that he had written his name – albeit reluctantly – down for one of her dances. "Of course. Forgive me, I quite forgot."

This did nothing other than dampen Lady Vivian's smile all the more. When Jonathan offered her his arm, she took it without a word, and they walked to the center of the room in silence. Jonathan did not care about their lack of conversation, not when he knew just how conniving and cunning she had been. He wanted her to understand, one way or the other, that there was to be no future for them, regardless of just how much she desired it.

"Let us join this set."

Waiting until she released his arm, Jonathan stepped back into his place and kept his smile fixed, already growing a little impatient for the music to begin. Forced to wait for the remaining couples to find their place, he let his gaze rove over the crowd of guests, wondering just where Miss Fullerton might now be.

"Are you looking for someone in particular?"

Lady Vivian's sharp question cut through his thoughts, and it took Jonathan something of an effort to keep his voice steady and calm.

"A little earlier this evening, I was informed that my mother had taken ill," he answered, throwing her a quick glance. "Fortunately, as I was on my way to the parlor where she was meant to be, I was waylaid and, thereafter, found her quite well." Lifting one eyebrow gently, he spread his hands. "I am questioning now who might have lied about such a thing, and what their purpose was for doing so."

"Mayhap it was Miss Fullerton."

Jonathan recoiled physically.

"I beg your pardon?"

"It would be a very strange thing for her to do, certainly, but mayhap there is a reason for such an action."

"Such as?" Jonathan spread his hands, waiting for her to suggest something, but Lady Vivian only smiled. Letting out a breath of frustration, Jonathan glared at the orchestra, as though they were deliberately refusing to play so that this conversation might continue regardless. "I feel that is a flawed concept if you cannot make even a suggestion as to her motivations."

Lady Vivian shrugged, her lips tugging to one side.

"Mayhap she hoped to entrap you."

"That is not in her nature."

"But if her father has turned his back on her, and with the Season soon drawing to a close, she likely has no other choice but to find a husband in whatever way she can! Your mother's generosity will not last for another Season, surely?" The music began and Lady Vivian dropped into a grand curtsey. "And her father's ignorance of the situation here at present certainly will not."

Jonathan's stomach dropped. Lady Vivian had spoken of Miss Fullerton's father on many occasions but this time, there appeared to be something of a threat there.

"As I have said, I have no concerns as regards Miss Fullerton's presence here in London and my mother's wisdom in hiring her," he stated, bowing rather sharply. "If I am frank, I find the suggestion of her guilt to be quite preposterous."

His hands balled into fists as he quelled the burning fire

in the pit of his stomach. Lady Vivian was more devious than he had ever imagined, for now she was attempting to place her guilt onto the shoulders of Miss Fullerton! Did she hope that, in doing so, Jonathan would turn away entirely from Miss Fullerton and, instead, pull Lady Vivian herself into his arms? His lip curled. The lady was most disagreeable, and he could hardly wait for the dance to be at an end so that he might remove himself from her company.

The lady said nothing more, and the dance continued in silence. Jonathan did not so much as glance at her, refusing to allow his gaze to land upon hers. Keeping his chin up, he breathed a sigh of relief when the music ended, and dance finally came to a close.

"I should be very careful around Miss Fullerton, Lord Havisham." Lady Vivian took his arm unbidden, her fingers tight. "You know that I say such things only out of concern for you, do you not? I cannot think of you and your reputation being so injured."

Jonathan shook his head.

"I have no need for your concern, Lady Vivian."

Her hand pulled from his and she swung around to face him, her eyes narrowed and flashing with anger.

"You throw my concern for you back in my face?"

"No." Jonathan took in a breath before he continued, fighting back the urge to simply turn on his heel and leave her standing there alone. "I do not fling it back at you, Lady Vivian, but I do not consider it. There is no need to do so. I know Miss Fullerton. I think her the finest creature in all of London, in fact, and thus have no need to worry."

Lady Vivian took a step back as though he had struck her.

"The finest creature in all of London?" she repeated, as Jonathan nodded. "You put her above me?"

"I put her above everyone, such is my regard for her," Jonathan answered, not hesitating for a moment. He saw the flash of understanding in Lady Vivian's eyes as color ran from her cheeks, leaving her pale. It seemed that she now realized exactly what he meant by such statement and Jonathan, for his part, was glad of it. "I think I shall take my leave, Lady Vivian."

Bowing, he waited until Lady Catherine had drawn near to Lady Vivian so that she would not be left standing entirely alone, and then turned away, satisfied. Lady Vivian now knew the truth about his feelings towards Miss Fullerton and that, he hoped, would be enough to push her away from him entirely.

CHAPTER FIFTEEN

"Are you ready?"

Deborah smoothed both hands down her skirts and nodded. Her stomach had been flooded with butterflies ever since the moment she had woken and the feeling lingered still, making her feel rather unsettled.

Lord Havisham had not come to speak to her as he had promised. Last evening had been a very late affair indeed, and by the time they had returned to the townhouse, the first light of dawn had been spreading across the horizon. Deborah had shared many looks with Lord Havisham, but nothing had been said – although when he had taken her hand to help her alight from the carriage, Deborah had hardly been able to breathe.

However, since breaking her fast, she had not seen Lord Havisham and, upon his mother's inquiry, had been informed that he was still abed. Now both she and Lady Havisham were to go to Lord Brecham's home to take tea with him and whoever else he had invited, and yet all Deborah wanted to do was remain exactly where she was until Lord Havisham appeared.

"This is to be an afternoon soiree, I am sure of it." Lady Havisham tutted as she turned towards the door, which was immediately opened for her by a waiting footman. "Lord Brecham did not call it so explicitly, but that is what it sounds like." Her eyes darted back towards Deborah as she turned her head over her shoulder. "Do you intend to join me, Miss Fullerton?"

Deborah flushed, pulled from her thoughts by Lady Havisham's gently teasing tone.

"Yes, of course."

Making her way outside, she sat down opposite Lady Havisham but kept her gaze trained on the door, waiting for Lord Havisham to appear... but he did not. And as the carriage rolled away, Deborah's hopes faded.

"You were waiting for my son, I think." Opening her mouth to respond, Deborah closed it again as Lady Havisham smiled knowingly. "He has come to realize the beauty that is before him, then?"

"I – I cannot say, Lady Havisham."

For the first time, Deborah realized that what Lady Havisham had said to her last evening about having particular gentlemen notice her might well have related to Lord Havisham. Had Lady Havisham already been aware of Lord Havisham's feelings?

"I am certain that he will have risen by the time we return," came the comforting reply. "There is a great joy in my heart over this, Miss Fullerton." Her smile lit her eyes and Deborah could not help but return it with one of her own. "I think my son has finally come to his senses!"

Deborah laughed, her cheeks still warm.

"It has been quite extraordinary. Although..." Her smile cracked and a frown pulled at her brow. "My father is not something we have discussed as yet."

Lady Havisham waved a hand.

"That will not concern him, my dear. I know my son. He will trust your word and mine also." Her smile grew. "I look forward to calling you my daughter-in-law!"

Deborah's blush grew hotter.

"There is no mention of that at present."

"Ah, but there soon will be," came the decisive reply. "Just wait, Miss Fullerton. It will not be long."

⁓

THOSE WORDS LINGERED in Deborah's heart as she sat quietly to take tea with Lady Brecham and the other ladies who had been invited for the afternoon. Lady Havisham had been correct to state that it was an afternoon soiree, for the gentlemen were busy drinking brandy and whisky whilst talking in loud tones in various parts of the drawing-room and parlor, whilst the ladies sat down with their tea and attempted to make quiet conversation. Deborah paid very little attention to anything which was being said, her thoughts still fixed on Lord Havisham. After their kiss, she had found the rest of the ball dull and lifeless, compared to all that she had felt when he had pulled her close. Even now, just the thought of it sent her heart clattering against her chest.

Deborah smiled.

"Ah, good afternoon, Miss Fullerton."

Looking up, Deborah rose quickly as Lord Harrogate came to stand beside her.

"Good afternoon, Lord Harrogate."

Deborah pressed her lips together, wondering how she might inform him that her heart was now quite engaged to another and that thus, his attempt to encourage her affections was doomed to failure.

"And where is Lord Havisham this afternoon?"

"I believe he is still resting," Deborah answered, gesturing to Lady Havisham. "I am sure that his mother would know a little more, should you wish to enquire of her."

Lord Harrogate grinned.

"No, indeed! I am glad that he is not here, else I fear that he would attempt to end our conversation in much the same way that he ended your dancing with Lord Thornley!"

"I believe he had his reasons."

"I am certain that he did not. No such reasons shall satisfy a gentleman who is so eagerly and obviously keen for a particular young lady's company." He leaned closer but Deborah moved back a fraction, not wanting to encourage him in any way. "Should you like to take a turn about the room?"

"No, thank you." Deborah did not hold back from refusing, seeing the way his smile shattered and his brow furrowed. "Lord Harrogate, you have been very kind in seeking out my company, but I must inform you that I have no intention of pursuing you in any way."

A small exclamation of delight came from behind her, and she turned sharply, wondering who it might be, just as Lord Thornley sped past her and came to join Lord Harrogate, who was looking decidedly disappointed.

"Lord... Thornley?" Deborah bobbed a quick curtsey, having not seen the gentleman present thus far. "Good afternoon."

"Good afternoon." Lord Thornley was beaming at her as though she had made him the happiest gentleman in all of London. "I am sorry to hear that you do not wish to incline yourself towards Lord Harrogate. Might I ask... you will think me most improper, but I cannot help but hope."

Deborah blinked.

"Hope?"

"Well...," Lord Thornley sounded hesitant, no longer looking directly at her. "I had hoped that, with your lack of interest in Lord Harrogate, there might be a specific interest in... someone else?"

Fire flared up into her face, but Deborah did not immediately reply. It could not be Lord Havisham that he meant but rather himself, in which case she would have to speak openly and honestly with him also.

"I had been considering you, Lord Thornley, yes," she admitted, at which Lord Thornley grinned with evident delight. "But I confess to you also that my heart is engaged elsewhere."

His grin disappeared in an instant.

"I beg your pardon?"

"I – I do not know how to put it more plainly," Deborah replied, now growing a trifle embarrassed. "You have been very kind to me indeed – both of you, in fact – and I very much appreciate your consideration. However, if I am honest, I find that my heart is quite lost to another and therefore –"

"He told you of our bet, did he not?"

Deborah stared at Lord Harrogate, completely flummoxed.

"Bet?"

The man snorted, crossing his arms over his chest as his lip curled.

"You need not pretend, Miss Fullerton."

"I am not, I assure you. I have no knowledge of this bet."

The heat which had been within her now began to

dampen as her embarrassment turned to shame as she looked from Lord Harrogate to Lord Thornley and realized that this bet had been to do with her.

"I am sure that Lord Havisham informed you of this," Lord Thornley's voice was filled with a furious anger that seemed to fill the room. "I threatened to reveal all that we knew about Lady Ensley, but it seems even that did not convince him."

"Lady Ensley?" Deborah repeated, but her breathless whisper was torn away from her as the two gentlemen continued to talk.

"Then there must be a fulfillment of your threat, Thornley. If Lord Havisham has told her the truth and she now pretends to know nothing of it, then –"

"She does not know anything of it." Deborah turned, just as Lord Havisham's hand caught her arm. "And shall we perhaps lower our voices, unless it is that you wish for every single gentleman of the *ton* to know about your foolishness?"

For whatever reason, this statement seemed to blow away both Lord Harrogate and Lord Thornley's bluster, for they both dropped their heads and muttered something under their breath.

"Miss Fullerton, I apologize for my absence this morning." Lord Havisham's hand was still on her arm, but when she looked up into his face, there was nothing but gravity there. "I had wanted to speak to you before the afternoon soiree, but I slept overlong. Perhaps it is because my heart contains such a great deal of happiness given what we shared yesterday." A tiny smile pulled at one side of his mouth and Deborah returned it, still very unsure of what was going on. "However, given that these two *fine* gentlemen have already spoken to you, it seems that I must tell you the truth." The irony of his words was not lost upon Lord Thornley and Lord Harrogate, for they grimaced and looked away, their jaws jutting forward. "I have been a coward, Miss Fullerton."

Deborah blinked at him, a tight hand grasping her heart. "I do not understand."

"Some time ago, I had an association with one Lady Ensley. At the time, I believed her widowed, for that was what she told me. It was something of a tawdry affair, and is something I now regret. However, it became clear that she was *not* widowed, as she had said, but rather that her husband had been at his estate while she was in London." This was all said in a low voice, but Deborah felt as though it were being shouted so that everyone in the house could hear him. "At that point, I ended our acquaintance entirely and, much to my relief, the *ton* did not come to know of it. Lord Harrogate, being my friend, knew of the lady and what had taken place, but swore that he would not say anything." His jaw worked for a moment. "However, it seems that when he has imbibed too much, he then speaks of what he ought not to – and Lord Thornley uses that to his advantage."

This was all becoming a little overwhelming and Deborah took in three long breaths before she asked something more. Closing her eyes, she straightened her shoulders and then looked directly at Lord Thornley.

"And this relates somehow to the bet that you made with Lord Harrogate?"

Lord Thornley grimaced and looked away, clearly refusing to answer.

"If you will not tell her, then I shall do so." Lord Havisham spread his hands. "Surely one of you has enough courage!"

The taunt was enough to loosen Lord Harrogate's tongue.

"I made a bet with Lord Thornley that *I* could gain your affections first."

"And whoever did not succeed would be required to pay the agreed amount," Lord Thornley interjected, angrily. "But Lord Havisham discovered it and wanted very much to tell you about it."

Lord Havisham's hand came back to her arm, drawing Deborah's attention.

"It was not because I did not think you could be happy with Lord Thornley but rather because I discovered that the bet was only about stealing your affections. They would not, thereafter, seek to court you or wed you. It was only about the money."

Deborah's eyes closed as a heavy weight settled itself on her heart. In Lord Thornley and Lord Harrogate's eyes, she was naught but a lowly creature able to be used for their own purposes rather than giving a fig for what she would feel or endure.

"I see."

"Thornley threatened to tell everyone about Lady Ensley. That ought not to have been enough of an impetus to keep me silent, but it was." Lord Havisham turned to face her a little more and Deborah swallowed hard as she looked up at him, blinking back hot tears. "That was wrong of me, Miss Fullerton, and I can only apologize."

She nodded stiffly, a lump aching in her throat.

"That was why you did not want me to dance with Lord Thornley?"

"Precisely. I could not – I *thought* that I could not tell you the truth, but I could prevent Lord Thornley from encouraging your affections one way or the other. Unfortunately, I ended up injuring you instead." He spread one hand out wide whilst still pressing her arm with the other. "I am truly sorry, Miss Fullerton. I did not do right in this situation, and I can only offer you my sincere apologies."

Everything now had become quite clear: the reason for his sudden change of heart as regarded her dancing, the strange manner in which he had behaved thereafter and the anger in his expression whenever he had looked at Lord Thornley.

"I wanted to protect you, but I also wanted to protect myself," Lord Havisham murmured, his shoulders dropping. "Yet the more I considered it, the more I came to realize that it was not what I wanted to do. If you recall, I *did* want to speak with you on certain matters, but we were simply not granted the time required for such a thing! Although, given the importance of the matter, I ought to have made it my priority."

"I understand why you did not want to tell me about the bet." Deborah lifted one shoulder, then dropped it again. "There are always things in one's past that one wishes to keep hidden." Her heart squeezed painfully as she thought of her father, knowing that, as yet, Lord Havisham did not know the truth in its entirety. "You need not apologize anymore."

She did not smile, but there was no heaviness in her chest any longer. In fact, there was something of a relief in finally understanding it all.

"I am sure that there are many things *you* would wish to keep hidden from Lord Havisham."

Another voice chimed in, and Deborah closed her eyes, clenching her teeth hard. For whatever reason, Lady Vivian had decided to interject herself into the conversation when she was unwelcome, and her input entirely unwarranted.

"We do not require your presence, Lady Vivian."

Lord Havisham's voice was hard, but it seemed as though the lady was determined to ignore him, for she came to stand directly opposite Deborah, tilting her head gently and lifting one eyebrow in question. Deborah drew in a long breath, set her shoulders, and lifted her chin.

Would Lady Vivian never leave her alone?

CHAPTER SIXTEEN

*T*elling Miss Fullerton the truth – whilst difficult – had brought Jonathan a great deal of relief. The heaviness which had wrapped around his heart like a heavy weight was gone, although he marveled at Miss Fullerton's understanding. She could easily have held his poor choices against him but instead, she had responded with kindness and generosity of spirit.

All the more reason to think well of her.

"I am sure that there are many things *you* would wish to keep hidden from Lord Havisham."

A surge of irritation raced through him, his skin prickling.

"We do not require your presence, Lady Vivian." He did not hold back from speaking with great frankness. There was enough to consider at present without Lady Vivian's spiteful presence. "Lord Thornley, Lord Harrogate, I believe that your bet is quite at an end." With a sidelong glance, he saw Lady Vivian come to stand directly opposite Miss Fullerton, making no attempt to remove herself from their company. "Miss Fullerton has not given her affections to either of you – and I have not said anything to her as regards the bet, so I cannot be asked to pay anything either."

Lord Thornley grimaced.

"That is entirely unfair. You have done all you can to steal Miss Fullerton's affections for yourself, knowing that this is the only way to end our bet! Is that not so?"

Jonathan spread his hands, releasing Miss Fullerton.

"I have done nothing of the sort."

"Indeed, he has not." Miss Fullerton's voice was quiet, but her words clear. "I have been struggling with my own feelings for some time, but it was not until yesterday that–"

"You mean to say that you *return* such feelings?" Lord Thornley interrupted, turning disbelieving eyes onto Jonathan. "Good gracious, I thought you a little wiser than that!"

Anger burned hot in Jonathan's cheeks and, whilst he did not immediately respond, the glower he sent in Lord Thornley's direction was enough to silence the man. Another quick glance towards Miss Fullerton showed Jonathan that she was a little red in the face, but still with her head held high. Unconsciously, he moved a little closer, wanting to be near her.

"I see nothing unwise in attaching myself to the daughter of a Viscount."

Lord Thornley's lip curled into a sneer, but it was Lady Vivian who spoke next.

"But what if she is *not* the daughter of a Viscount?"

Miss Fullerton's gasp seemed to echo around the room and Jonathan became slowly aware that there were many others in the room who were now listening to what was being said. The anger which had curled through his veins initially now burst into a furious ball of heat and rage and he took a step forward, ready to speak to her in such a way that Lady Vivian would never dream of talking of Miss Fullerton again.

"You do not believe me?" Lady Vivian looked up at him without any flicker of hesitation in her eyes, her lips curved into a smirk. "I have no fear of your response, Lord Havisham, for it will die away the very moment you look into Miss Fullerton's face."

Jonathan's whole body was tight with anger, his brows knotted together.

"I care not, Lady Vivian," he hissed, as she continued to smile in that most infuriating way. "If she were the daughter of a pauper, I would not care!"

"Are you quite certain?" Her sing song voice grated on him all the more. "This young lady has not told you the truth, Lord Havisham! She is not the daughter of a Viscount. She is a disgraced, tarnished creature who ought not to be permitted even to *stand* next to you."

"That is enough, if you please." Miss Fullerton's voice was shaking terribly but, as he looked back at her, Jonathan saw the paleness of her cheeks and the way she blinked furiously. *Can there be any truth in what Lady Vivian has said?* "I have never lied to Lord Havisham." Miss Fullerton gazed fixedly at Lady Vivian whose smile faltered for the first time. "I have not told him all that there is to know about my father, because there is no need to do so – and this on the direction of Lady Havisham also. She is aware of it all and has encouraged me throughout to make very little of the matter."

"Your father does not know that you are here in London, presenting yourself as an eligible young lady, does he?" Lady Vivian planted both hands on her hips, her eyes narrowing. "That is something which has been deliberately kept from him."

"It has." Miss Fullerton shrugged one shoulder. "Although I cannot see why such a thing would concern you."

Lady Vivian's hand flung out towards Jonathan.

"Because you are attempting to steal the heart of one of London's most eligible gentlemen! It is not right that someone such as *you* should do such a thing! A gentleman of Lord Havisham's standing ought to wed someone a good deal more suitable."

Jonathan cleared his throat.

"I think that *I* can decide who or what is best for me, or the most suitable for me, Lady Vivian." He gestured towards Miss Fullerton. "Which, as you can see, is exactly what I have done in choosing to pursue Miss Fullerton."

"But you do not know the truth about her!" Lady Vivian exclaimed, drawing the attention of many of the other guests. "Her father does not want her! He does not even acknowledge her any longer."

"Then there should be no concern on my part that he will cause any difficulties for our future," Jonathan quipped, trying hard to bring the conversation to an end. "I thank you for your concern, Lady Vivian, but it is not required."

He did not understand fully all that Lady Vivian was saying and certainly did not know why Miss Fullerton's father did not acknowledge her, but that was not something which he needed to discuss at this present moment. That could be discussed just between Miss Fullerton and himself at a later, more private, opportunity. He did not want to prolong the conversation here any further, not with so many other people listening in.

Lady Vivian threw up her hands.

"Miss Fullerton is not Lord Ingleby's legitimate daughter!"

Her exclamation seemed to bring the room to a standstill. Jonathan closed his eyes briefly, his heart slamming hard against his chest as he waited for the murmur of conversation to begin again. Opening his eyes, he glanced at Miss Fullerton and saw that she had not moved an inch. Her eyes were still fixed on Lady Vivian, her hands clasped lightly in front of her – but her face was sheet white.

"Is that you, Lady Vivian?"

The sharp voice of Lady Havisham cut across the room and Jonathan turned to permit her entry into their small group.

"I know that you are eager to wed my son but there is no reason to speak lies about Miss Fullerton in a vain attempt to gain what you will never have!" Lady Havisham's voice was calm and clear and, yet again, the murmuring around them came to a slow stop. Everyone in the room was listening to what Lady Havisham had to say and Jonathan was suddenly very grateful indeed for his mother's presence. "My son has made his choice, Lady Vivian. In case you are unaware, Miss Fullerton is the lady he has come to care for. They are now courting."

Jonathan heard the surprise run around the room between the onlookers but kept his face set, taking another small step closer to Miss Fullerton and, even though it was not the expected thing for any gentleman to do, putting his hand out to catch hers. Her fingers were ice cold, and he squeezed her hand gently, in an attempt to reassure her. Miss Fullerton did not so much as glance at him.

"Miss Fullerton came as my companion, yes, but I can assure you, Lady Vivian, her father is very much aware of her situation and standing. I am astonished to hear such falsehoods from you! You are a lady of quality, and for you to spread such rumors and slander is quite beyond the pale."

She gestured towards Jonathan, and he caught the redness in her face. His mother was clearly very angry. "My son will not be your husband, Lady Vivian, and I am certain we would all appreciate it if you could remain silent about any matters relating to him and Miss Fullerton in the future."

Part of him wanted to applaud his mother's remarks but Jonathan settled for smiling broadly instead. Lady Vivian, however, did not quail before Lady Havisham as he had expected. Her shoulders did not drop, her gaze did not fall to the ground and, indeed, she did not show even the smallest sign of embarrassment.

"You may say as much as you please about Lord Ingleby's awareness of Miss Fullerton's situation, such as it stands, but I am certain that what you claim is not the case. Indeed, I have written to Lord Ingleby, informing him that Miss Fullerton is seeking to arrange a marriage for herself and received only this morning a very short but appreciative note in return." She smiled, the coldness in her eyes sending a chill down Jonathan's back. "From what I understand, the uncertainty around Miss Fullerton's birth has left Lord Ingleby determined that she will not achieve the rank she *supposedly* ought to hold, given that she is – most likely – not a lady of quality at all!"

Jonathan could not listen to another word. Miss Fullerton's hand had tightened on his with practically every word Lady Vivian had said, and whether or not any of it was true, he did not want to have her injured any further. He should have put a stop to Lady Vivian's determined conversation long before now.

"That is quite enough." His voice rang through the room, filled with a severity which forced the smile from Lady Vivian's face. "How dare you speak so? This is utterly preposterous, and I find the fact that you are attempting to speak untruths about the lady I am now *courting* to be deeply upsetting. Were you a gentleman, then I would call you out for such behavior!"

Lady Vivian's face whitened.

"Whatever is the meaning of this?"

In a trice, Lady Havisham had caught the attention of Lady Vivian's mother, the Countess of Marlock, who had suddenly appeared next to her daughter's side. Before Lady Vivian could say a word in her own defense, Lady Havisham explained all.

"I am afraid, Lady Marlock, that your daughter has been speaking both unkindly and falsely about my companion, Miss Fullerton." She gestured to Miss Fullerton, who raised her chin a fraction, although she herself remained quite silent. "There are untruths being spoken about her legitimacy as Lord Ingleby's daughter, which my son, given that he is now courting Miss Fullerton, will not tolerate. And nor will I, for that matter."

"She has spoken of these things with such a loud voice that the entirety of this room has heard every word," Jonathan informed Lady Marlock, who was now herself going puce. "As I have said, I am now courting Miss Fullerton and I am greatly upset at such rumors being spread! I confess myself to be deeply offended, Lady Marlock, and beg that you take your daughter away for the moment and, at a suitable time thereafter, have her apologize to Miss Fullerton *and* to myself."

It was as if the whole room held its breath, waiting for Lady Marlock's response. Either she could state that Jonathan had no right to demand such things, and come to her daughter's defense, or she could immediately do as he had asked and remove Lady Vivian from the room. The latter would ensure that the rest of those present believed that Miss Fullerton had been severely wronged by Lady Vivian, whereas the former might convince them that something, indeed, was amiss between Lord Ingleby and his daughter.

Taking a deep breath, Lady Marlock raised her hand and settled it on her daughter's shoulder. Lady Vivian looked towards her mother and then turned her gaze back towards Jonathan. A small, triumphant smile settled across her face and Jonathan's heart sank.

"I am deeply sorry, Lord Havisham, for what my daughter has done. I am deeply ashamed to hear of what she has done and unspeakably angry at the shame she has brought on her name and on that of her father and myself." Jonathan let out a surreptitious breath of relief, keeping his stance tall and his expression somewhat dark. "I will depart at this very moment, and you can be certain that an apology will be given very soon indeed." Lady Marlock looked down at her daughter and Jonathan also turned his gaze to Lady Vivian. It appeared that there was something of shock in Lady Vivian over the response from her mother, for her eyes were wide and her mouth a little ajar. "Vivian?"

Lady Marlock's tone brooked no argument and, after a few moments, Lady Vivian bowed her head, her shoulders slumping in defeat.

"Yes, of course, Mama."

"I can only beg your forgiveness, Miss Fullerton," Lady Marlock continued, gesturing to the young lady. "May I take this moment to wish your courtship success. I know that you will have made many young ladies very envious indeed."

She shot a hard look to her daughter, and then without another word, stepped away. Lady Vivian followed in her wake, her head drooping and all sense of victory quite gone from her. The door opened and then was closed behind them and Jonathan let out a long sigh of relief, which was soon followed by a good many others in the room.

"Miss Fullerton."

Turning to her and ignoring the hubbub of conversation which immediately began to grow within the room, he grasped both of her hands and looked down into her eyes.

They were filled with tears.

His heart ached for her. She had maintained her composure throughout the conversation with Lady Vivian and had not allowed her to see any sort of pain, not even for a single moment. But now that she was standing with him, in the absence of Lady Vivian and her mother, her true emotions were coming to the fore.

"You did remarkably well, my dear." Lady Havisham slipped one arm about Miss Fullerton's shoulders. "I should like to encourage you to return home, but I think that it would be best if we remained here at present. For a short while, at least."

Jonathan nodded his agreement.

"If you can manage a few short minutes, Miss Fullerton, then it would be best for you to remain. The present guests will be watching for your reaction and, if we depart in a hurry, they will think you angry and upset – and a good deal more gossip could come from that." He pressed her hands again, seeing her blink her tears away, swallowing hard as she did so. "What say you, Miss Fullerton? Are you able to remain? If you wish to depart then I will, of course, accompany you."

She took a moment but then nodded, swallowing tightly again.

"I can stay." Her voice was thin, but her eyes no longer held tears. "Thank you, Lord Havisham, Lady Havisham."

A smile was attempted but quickly faltered. "That was quite horrifying."

Jonathan nodded, then released one of her hands.

"I think that a good deal of gossip will be prevented, given Lady Marlock's reaction."

"I must hope so, although..." Closing her eyes tightly, Miss Fullerton drew in a shaky breath. "Lady Vivian stated that she wrote to my father. I am not certain that her statement was false."

Frowning, Jonathan glanced at his mother, only to see lines forming across her brow also. Clearly, there was something of grave concern in such a statement but, as yet, he did not understand it.

"Let us think upon such things once we are at home and you have recovered, Miss Fullerton." Lady Havisham's frown lingered, but her words were calming. "There is a good deal to consider, yes, but you must recover yourself. Your head will be much too muddled otherwise."

Jonathan smiled, nodding as Miss Fullerton opened her eyes and looked up at him.

"Shall I fetch you something to drink?"

"Yes, thank you."

Sharing a long look with his mother, Jonathan squeezed Miss Fullerton's hand once more.

"You are contented with my statement that we are now courting, I hope?"

This brought the most beautiful, warm smile to Miss Fullerton's lips that Jonathan had ever seen. It made his heart lift, joy pouring into his soul and pushing aside the confusion and fear which had been there only a few minutes ago.

"I am very contented, Lord Havisham. That is, if it is what you truly desire?"

"It is," he confirmed, as she lowered her eyes demurely although her smile still lingered. "And I consider myself to be the most fortunate of gentlemen, Miss Fullerton, to have been accepted by you." When she glanced up at him, Jonathan laughed at the pink in her cheeks. "Come now, let me leave you to the care of my mother and fetch us all something to drink. I will return shortly."

"Thank you, Lord Havisham." Her voice was soft, but her smile beautiful. Whatever it was as regarded her father, Jonathan was quite determined that they would overcome it. Nothing more would keep him from his future with Miss Fullerton.

CHAPTER SEVENTEEN

'*I have written to Lord Ingleby, informing him that Miss Fullerton is seeking to arrange a marriage for herself and received only this morning a very short but appreciative note in return.*'

Deborah closed her eyes and shuddered. Those words had not left her mind since they had first been spoken by Lady Vivian and even now, she felt them terrify her all over again. If Lady Vivian had received a note, then Deborah was quite certain that her father would not be long behind. He would want to make certain that she was no longer permitted to do as she had been, that she was not to be seen as a lady of quality. No doubt he would do all that he could to try to remove her from London entirely, and that would mean an end to her connection to Lord Havisham!

"Although, as Lady Havisham has engaged me as a companion and has paid father for my company," she told herself as she walked slowly towards the dining room, ready to break her fast. "If Lady Havisham has given him the required coin, then can he demand that I leave her house?"

The question did not answer itself, however, and

Deborah let out a heavy sigh, her forehead lined with confusion. Reaching the door, she took a deep breath and then set her shoulders, forcing a smile to her face.

Walking inside, Deborah stopped short at the sight of both Lady Havisham and Lord Havisham sitting together at the table. It was most unusual for Lord Havisham to be present for breaking their fast, given that he was usually still abed, although from the broad, welcoming smile on his face, he seemed to be delighted to be here at this early hour.

Deborah's smile grew, despite her warring confusion. When he had stated yesterday, in the course of conversation, that he was now courting her, Deborah had been caught up with both confusion and delight. It had taken her some time to believe that it was true, and that he truly *did* want to court her, but when he had confirmed it to her, Deborah's heart had never known such joy. The same joy she felt at simply being in his presence once more.

"Come and sit down, my dear."

Lady Havisham and Lord Havisham both rose from the table and Deborah hurried to join them, blushing just a little as Lord Havisham came to help her seat herself, rather than leaving it to one of the footmen. His hand brushed across her shoulder for a moment as he smiled down into her eyes.

"You look lovely this morning, my dear."

Her blush deepened, but she did not drop her gaze from his eyes.

"Thank you, Lord Havisham. I am glad to be back in your company this morning."

"As I am also, to be in yours."

His fingers pressed her shoulder lightly, but then he returned to his seat, his eyes still lingering on her as her heart quickened.

"You look fatigued, my dear." Lady Havisham gestured to one of the footmen, who quickly stepped forward to pour tea for Deborah, and then brought a piece of toast already buttered, just as she liked it. "We are all prepared for you, as you can see."

Deborah smiled her appreciation.

"I thank you."

"You will be glad to know, I think, that the gossip this morning centers solely on Lady Vivian, rather than on you."

Looking up, Deborah held fast to Lord Havisham's gaze, a knot in her chest.

"Oh?"

"There was always going to be gossip, my dear, but it is good that the *ton* have not thought ill of you. Lady Vivian will be expected to make a grand apology."

Deborah swallowed hard, letting out a slow breath. It was time to tell Lord Havisham the truth about her father.

"She is not entirely mistaken in all that she said, Lord Havisham." Seeing his brows lift, Deborah closed her eyes in mortification. "My father has never outright refused to acknowledge me. However, he has always insisted that he could not be certain of my mother's devotion to him. I believe around the time of my conception, there was a particular friendship between my mother and a gentleman who lived near our estate. My mother always denied such a thing, begging him to trust her, to believe her, but he was quite determined that she was guilty." Her cheeks were hot, but she forced herself to continue speaking regardless, opening her eyes but looking down at the table rather than at Lord Havisham. It needed all to be said, so that Lord Havisham was in no doubt as to her present situation. "It could never be proven, of course, but my father made it clear that he did not truly consider me his daughter –

stating this all the more when my mother passed away. Determined that I should never be treated as a lady of quality, he refused my request for a Season, and instead sought out a position for me as either a governess or companion." She gestured to Lady Havisham, who was smiling gently. "It is only due to your mother's kindness that I became *her* companion and, thereafter, was permitted to step forward into my place as a lady of society."

A short silence followed her words and Deborah dragged her gaze up towards Lord Havisham's face, afraid of what she would see there. His brow was furrowed, his lips tight and his jaw thrust forward.

Her head bowed again. He was angry with her. Angry that she had not told him all from the very beginning and mayhap even angry that he had tied himself to her without knowing the truth of her circumstances.

"How very cruel a gentleman he must be." Her eyes flew to his, widening in surprise as she realized that his anger was not directed at her, but rather towards her father. "To think so little of your mother – his wife – and then to treat you with that same unmerited disdain?" Lord Havisham shook his head, a slight redness coming into his face. "That is despicable."

A weakness rolled through her, such was her relief at his understanding, to the point that she had to lean forward and put one hand to her head, her elbow resting on the arm of the chair.

"You surely did not think that I would turn away from you?" she heard Lord Havisham say. "I am a changed man, Miss Fullerton, which has come about solely because of your presence in my home."

The soft scraping of a chair caught her ears and the next moment, his arms were around her, pulling her gently to stand so that he might hold her close. Deborah's eyes closed as she rested her head against his chest, feeling the steady beat of his heart. She was safe here, safe in his arms, and the threat of her father suddenly seemed to disappear.

"We must still take care." Lady Havisham's voice interrupted them, and Lord Havisham pulled back gently, although one arm still lingered around her waist. "If Lady Vivian has written to your father – which, I believe, she has done – then there is every possibility that Lord Ingleby will be in London within the next few days."

"Do you think it possible that he would attempt to take Miss Fullerton back to his estate?" Lord Havisham asked, as Deborah began to nod. "Even though we are courting?"

"I think that would be his sole purpose," Lady Havisham replied, as Deborah sighed heavily. "He does not want Miss Fullerton to gain any sort of standing, as she has mentioned."

"And I do not think that my employment will make any difference."

Lord Havisham let out a long breath.

"Then I must depart."

Deborah's head swiveled towards him.

"Depart?"

"I must make some arrangements!" Lord Havisham grinned suddenly, confusing her all the more with his seeming delight at this possible dark occurrence. "Have no fear, Miss Fullerton, you need not worry about your father. There is going to be nothing to concern you any longer, I assure you. I will return very soon."

Swallowing her confusion, Deborah tried to nod.

"Very well."

His lips brushed her forehead, his hands catching both of hers, squeezing them gently.

"Do you trust me, Deborah?"

It was the first time he had said her name and Deborah's heart lifted with warmth and delight.

"I do trust you, yes."

"Then trust that I will return soon, and that all will be well."

She smiled, looking up into his eyes.

"I look forward to your return, Havisham."

∽

"Miss Fullerton." Deborah jerked awake from her doze, a little embarrassed to have been caught so. Lady Havisham smiled gently but did not move away from the door. "Come." Rising from her chair a little unsteadily, Deborah's heart began to quicken as she came towards Lady Havisham. "It seems that my greatest hope has been achieved, my dear," she said, as Deborah listened in breathless anticipation, aware that there was something of significance about to take place, but having no understanding as to what that might be. "If you would make your way to the front door, he will be waiting for you."

She grasped Deborah's hand for a moment, then held out one hand into the hallway, as if guiding her through. Tears began to burn in Deborah's eyes, but she blinked them away, feeling a great sense of excited expectation beginning to burn in her heart. With hurried steps, she made her way down the staircase and to the front of the house, her breath catching as Lord Havisham turned towards her.

She was in his arms in a moment, clinging to him as though she could never let him go. Lord Havisham held her tightly, his lips close to her ear as he murmured to her, comforting her, thanking her for trusting him.

"I have returned, as I promised." His breath whispered across her cheek, and Deborah shivered, lifting her head to look up into his eyes. "I know that you have been waiting for many hours. I do hope you have eaten?"

"Dinner was a few hours ago." A little concerned, she put one hand on his chest. "Did you expect us to wait for you?"

Laughing, Lord Havisham shook his head.

"No, indeed not. I wanted to make sure that *you* would not be overly hungry on our long journey. That is all."

Her eyes flared.

"Long journey?"

"Yes." His voice softened, one hand cupping her chin. "I have thought about the dangers which lie before us as regards your father. If he should come to London as you expect, then he might very well attempt to remove you from my arms. Thus, to make certain that does not happen, we must find a way to make certain he cannot."

A little confused, Deborah said nothing, waiting for him to explain. Lord Havisham smiled, his eyes gleaming like emeralds, his fair hair falling over his forehead as he bent his head low.

"I thought that we should make our way to Scotland. There is only one way to keep your father from taking you back home, and that is to make you my wife."

Deborah stared at him, hardly able to take it in. Was she to become Lord Havisham's wife?

"You have not said a word!" Lord Havisham laughed, pulling her even closer. "Pray do not say that you will refuse me? Not when I have fallen so deeply in love with you!" His smile softened as he spoke, and Deborah heard the truth in every single word. She could not take it in; it was all far too wonderful. To know that this gentleman had come to love her in the same way that she cared for him was more than astonishing and yet the joy and happiness that filled her told her that it was true. "Deborah?"

Her eyes closed and she leaned into him, her head on his chest, listening to the steady thrum of his heart.

"I love you."

His lips brushed the top of her forehead and Deborah lifted her head in response, her eyes still closed. The gentle heat of his lips on her own sent tremors of delight through her frame as he caught her hand, resting it gently against his heart.

"You will marry me?"

She smiled against his mouth, dazed with all that she felt.

"I will."

"Then there is no time to waste." Before she could respond, he bent low and, one hand under her knees, lifted her cleanly off her feet. Deborah laughed and put her arms around his neck, seeing the way that his eyes danced.

"The carriage is ready and waiting. My mother has packed a valise for you." Turning his head a little more, he leaned down and caught her lips again in a quick kiss, making Deborah sigh with contentment. "You shall never be fearful again, Deborah. Never be treated as though you are worthless. In my eyes, you are the most beautiful, wonderful, and marvelous creature I have ever known – and I intend to make certain that you feel that every single day."

Deborah smiled and dropped her head onto his shoulder as he held her close, walking through the door and down the stone steps to the carriage. She had nothing to fear any longer. Lord Havisham had saved her with his love and Deborah could do nothing other than love him in return.

I HOPE you enjoyed Deborah's story. I am glad Lord Havisham turned out so much better than what he originally appeared! If you missed the first book in the Ladies on their Own series, check out More Than a Companion. Read ahead for a sneak peak of the story!

MY DEAR READER

Thank you for reading and supporting my books! I hope this story brought you some escape from the real world into the always captivating Regency world. A good story, especially one with a happy ending, just brightens your day and makes you feel good! If you enjoyed the book, would you leave a review on Amazon? Reviews are always appreciated.

Below is a complete list of all my books! Why not click and see if one of them can keep you entertained for a few hours?

The Duke's Daughters Series
The Duke's Daughters: A Sweet Regency Romance Boxset
A Rogue for a Lady
My Restless Earl
Rescued by an Earl
In the Arms of an Earl
The Reluctant Marquess (Prequel)

A Smithfield Market Regency Romance
The Smithfield Market Romances: A Sweet Regency
Romance Boxset
The Rogue's Flower
Saved by the Scoundrel
Mending the Duke
The Baron's Malady

The Returned Lords of Grosvenor Square
The Returned Lords of Grosvenor Square: A Regency Romance Boxset
The Waiting Bride
The Long Return
The Duke's Saving Grace
A New Home for the Duke

The Spinsters Guild
The Spinsters Guild: A Sweet Regency Romance Boxset
A New Beginning
The Disgraced Bride
A Gentleman's Revenge
A Foolish Wager
A Lord Undone

Convenient Arrangements
Convenient Arrangements: A Regency Romance Collection
A Broken Betrothal
In Search of Love
Wed in Disgrace
Betrayal and Lies
A Past to Forget
Engaged to a Friend

Landon House
Mistaken for a Rake
A Selfish Heart
A Love Unbroken
A Christmas Match
A Most Suitable Bride
An Expectation of Love

Second Chance Regency Romance
Loving the Scarred Soldier
Second Chance for Love
A Family of her Own
A Spinster No More

Soldiers and Sweethearts
To Trust a Viscount
Whispers of the Heart
Dare to Love a Marquess
Healing the Earl
A Lady's Brave Heart

Ladies on their Own: Governesses and Companions
More Than a Companion
The Hidden Governess
The Companion and the Earl

Christmas Stories
Love and Christmas Wishes: Three Regency Romance Novellas
A Family for Christmas
Mistletoe Magic: A Regency Romance
Heart, Homes & Holidays: A Sweet Romance Anthology

Happy Reading!

All my love,

Rose

A SNEAK PEEK OF MORE THAN A COMPANION

PROLOGUE

"Did you hear me, Honora?"

Miss Honora Gregory lifted her head at once, knowing that her father did not refer to her as 'Honora' very often and that he only did so when he was either irritated or angry with her.

"I do apologize, father, I was lost in my book," Honora replied, choosing to be truthful with her father rather than make excuses, despite the ire she feared would now follow. "Forgive my lack of consideration."

This seemed to soften Lord Greene just a little, for his scowl faded and his lips were no longer taut.

"I shall only repeat myself the once," her father said firmly, although there was no longer that hint of frustration in his voice. "There is very little money, Nora. I cannot give you a Season."

All thought of her book fled from Honora's mind as her eyes fixed to her father's, her chest suddenly tight. She had known that her father was struggling financially, although she had never been permitted to be aware of the details. But not to have a Season was deeply upsetting, and Honora had to immediately fight back hot tears which sprang into her eyes. There had always been a little hope in her heart, had always been a flicker of expectation that, despite knowing her father's situation, he might still be able to take her to London."

"Your aunt, however, is eager to go to London," Lord Greene continued, as Honora pressed one hand to her stomach in an attempt to soothe the sudden rolling and writhing which had captured her. He waved a hand dismissively, his expression twisting. "I do not know the reasons for it, given that she is widowed and, despite that, happily settled, but it seems she is determined to have some time in London this summer. Therefore, whilst you are not to have a Season of your own – you will not be presented or the like – you will go with your aunt to London."

Honora swallowed against the tightness in her throat, her hands twisting at her gown as she fought against a myriad of emotions.

"I am to be her companion?" she said, her voice only just a whisper as her father nodded.

She had always been aware that Lady Langdon, her aunt, had only ever considered her own happiness and her own situation, but to invite your niece to London as your companion rather than chaperone her for a Season surely spoke of selfishness!

"It is not what you might have hoped for, I know," her father continued, sounding resigned as a small sigh escaped his lips, his shoulders slumping. Honora looked up at him, seeing him now a little grey and realizing the full extent of his weariness. Some of her upset faded as she took in her father's demeanor, knowing that his lack of financial security was not his doing. The estate lands had done poorly these last three years, what with drought one year and flooding the next. As such, money had been ploughed into the ground to restore it and yet it would not become profitable again for at least another year. She could not blame her father for that. And yet, her heart had struggled against such news, trying to be glad that she would be in London but broken-hearted to learn that her aunt wanted her as her companion and nothing more. "I will not join you, of course," Lord Greene continued, coming a little closer to Honora and tilting his head just a fraction, studying his daughter carefully and, perhaps, all too aware of her inner turmoil. "You can, of course, choose to refuse your aunt's invitation – but I can offer you nothing more than what is being given to you at present, Nora. This may be your only opportunity to be in London."

Honora blinked rapidly against the sudden flow of hot tears that threatened to pour from her eyes, should she permit them.

"It is very good of my aunt," she managed to say, trying to be both gracious and thankful whilst ignoring the other, more negative feelings which troubled her. "Of course, I shall go."

Lord Greene smiled sadly, then reached out and settled one hand on Honora's shoulder, bending down just a little as he did so.

"My dear girl, would that I could give you more. You already have enough to endure, with the loss of your mother when you were just a child yourself. And now you have a poor father who cannot provide for you as he ought."

"I understand, Father," Honora replied quickly, not wanting to have her father's soul laden with guilt. "Pray, do not concern yourself. I shall be contented enough with what Lady Langdon has offered me."

Her father closed his eyes and let out another long sigh, accompanied this time with a shake of his head.

"She may be willing to allow you a little freedom, my dear girl," he said, without even the faintest trace of hope in his voice. "My sister has always been inclined to think only of herself, but there may yet be a change in her character."

Honora was still trying to accept the news that she was to be a companion to her aunt and could not make even a murmur of agreement. She closed her eyes, seeing a vision of herself standing in a ballroom, surrounded by ladies and gentlemen of the *ton*. She could almost hear the music, could almost feel the warmth on her skin... and then realized that she would be sitting quietly at the back of the room, able only to watch, and not to engage with any of it. Pain etched itself across her heart and Honora let out a long, slow breath, allowing the news to sink into her very soul.

"Thank you, Father." Her voice was hoarse but her words heartfelt, knowing that her father was doing his very best for her in the circumstances. "I will be a good companion for my aunt."

"I am sure that you will be, my dear," he said, quietly. "And I will pray that, despite everything, you might find a match – even in the difficulties that face us."

The smile faded from Honora's lips as, with that, her father left the room. There was very little chance of such a thing happening, as she was to be a companion rather than a debutante. The realization that she would be an afterthought, a lady worth nothing more than a mere glance from the moment that she set foot in London, began to tear away at Honora's heart, making her brow furrow and her lips pull downwards. There could be no moments of sheer enjoyment for her, no time when she was not considering all that was required of her as her aunt's companion. She would have to make certain that her thoughts were always fixed on her responsibilities, that her intentions were settled on her aunt at all times. Yes, there would be gentlemen to smile at and, on the rare chance, mayhap even converse with, but her aunt would not often permit such a thing, she was sure. Lady Langdon had her own reasons for going to London for the Season, whatever they were, and Honora was certain she would take every moment for herself.

"I must be grateful," Honora murmured to herself, setting aside her book completely as she rose from her chair and meandered towards the window.

Looking out at the grounds below, she took in the gardens, the pond to her right and the rose garden to her left. There were so many things here that held such beauty and, with it, such fond memories that there was a part of her, Honora had to admit, which did not want to leave it, did not want to set foot in London where she might find herself in a new and lower situation. There was security here, a comfort which encouraged her to remain, which told her to hold fast to all that she knew – but Honora was all too aware that she could not. Her future was not here. When her father passed away, if she was not wed, then Honora knew that she would be left to continue on as a companion, just to make certain that she had a home and enough coin for her later years. That was not the future she wanted but, she considered, it might very well be all that she could gain. Tears began to swell in her eyes, and she dropped her head, squeezing her eyes closed and forcing the tears back. This was the only opportunity she would have to go to London and, whilst it was not what she had hoped for, Honora had to accept it for what it was and begin to prepare herself for leaving her father's house – possibly, she considered, for good. Clasping both hands together, Honora drew in a long breath and let it out slowly as her eyes closed and her shoulders dropped.

A new part of her life was beginning. A new and unexpected future was being offered to her, and Honora had no other choice but to grasp it with both hands.

CHAPTER ONE

Pushing all doubt aside, Robert walked into White's with the air of someone who expected not only to be noticed, but to be greeted and exclaimed over in the most exaggerated manner. His chin lifted as he snapped his fingers towards one of the waiting footmen, giving him his request for the finest of brandies in short, sharp words. Then, he continued to make his way inside, his hands swinging loosely by his sides, his shoulders pulled back and his chest a little puffed out.

"Goodness, is that you?"

Robert grinned, his expectations seeming to be met, as a gentleman to his left rose to his feet and came towards him, only for him to stop suddenly and shake his head.

"Forgive me, you are not Lord Johnstone," he said, holding up both hands, palms out, towards Robert. "I thought that you were he, for you have a very similar appearance."

Grimacing, Robert shrugged and said not a word, making his way past the gentleman and finding a slight heat rising into his face. To be mistaken for another was one thing, but to remain entirely unrecognized was quite another! His doubts attempted to come rushing back. Surely someone would remember him, would remember what he had done last Season?

"Lord Crampton, good evening."

Much to his relief, Robert heard his title being spoken and turned his head to the right, seeing a gentleman sitting in a high-backed chair, a glass of brandy in his hand and a small smile on his face as he looked up at Robert.

"Good evening, Lord Marchmont," Robert replied, glad indeed that someone, at least, had recognized him. "I am back in London, as you can see."

"I hope you find it a pleasant visit," came the reply, only for Lord Marchmont to turn away and continue speaking to another gentleman sitting opposite – a man whom Robert had neither seen, nor was acquainted with. There was no suggestion from Lord Marchmont about introducing Robert to him and, irritated, Robert turned sharply away. His head dropped, his shoulders rounded, and he did not even attempt to keep his frustration out of his expression. His jaw tightened, his eyes blazed and his hands balled into fists.

Had they all forgotten him so quickly?

Practically flinging himself into a large, overstuffed armchair in the corner of White's, Robert began to mutter darkly to himself, almost angry about how he had been treated. Last Season he had been the talk of London! Why should he be so easily forgotten now? Unpleasant memories rose, of being inconspicuous, and disregarded, when he had first inherited his title. He attempted to push them aside, but his upset grew steadily so that even the brandy he was given by the footman – who had spent some minutes trying to find Lord Crampton – tasted like ash in his mouth. Nothing took his upset away and Robert wrapped it around his shoulders like a blanket, huddling against it and keeping it close to him.

He had not expected this. He had hoped to be not only remembered but celebrated! When he stepped into a room, he thought that he should be noticed. He *wanted* his name to be murmured by others, for it to be spread around the room that he had arrived! Instead, he was left with an almost painful frustration that he had been so quickly forgotten by the *ton* who, only a few months ago, had been his adoring admirers.

"Another brandy might help remove that look from your face." Robert did not so much as blink, hearing the man's voice but barely acknowledging it. "You are upset, I can tell." The man rose and came to sit opposite Robert, who finally was forced to recognize him. "That is no way for a gentleman to appear upon his first few days in London!"

Robert's lip curled. He should not, he knew, express his frustration so openly, but he found that he could not help himself.

"Good evening, Lord Burnley," he muttered, finding the man's broad smile and bright eyes to be nothing more than an irritation. "Are *you* enjoying the London Season thus far?"

Lord Burnley chuckled, his eyes dancing - which added to Robert's irritation all the more. He wanted to turn his head away, to make it plain to Lord Burnley that he did not enjoy his company and wanted very much to be free of it, but his standing as a gentleman would not permit him to do so.

"I have only been here a sennight but yes, I have found

a great deal of enjoyment thus far," Lord Burnley told him. "But you should expect that, should you not? After all, a gentleman coming to London for the Season comes for good company, fine wine, excellent conversation and to be in the company of beautiful young ladies – one of whom might even catch his eye!"

This was, of course, suggestive of the fact that Lord Burnley might have had his head turned already by one of the young women making their come out, but Robert was in no mood to enter such a discussion. Instead, he merely sighed, picked up his glass again and held it out to the nearby footman, who came over to them at once.

"Another," he grunted, as the man took his glass from him. "And for Lord Burnley here."

Lord Burnley chuckled again, the sound grating on Robert's skin.

"I am quite contented with what I have at present, although I thank you for your consideration," he replied, making Robert's brow lift in surprise. What sort of gentleman turned down the opportunity to drink fine brandy? Half wishing that Lord Burnley would take his leave so that he might sit here in silence and roll around in his frustration, Robert settled back in his chair, his arms crossed over his chest and his gaze turned away from Lord Burnley in the vain hope that this would encourage the man to take his leave. He realized that he was behaving churlishly, yet somehow, he could not prevent it – he had hoped so much, and so far, nothing was as he had expected. "So, you are returned to London," Lord Burnley said, making Robert roll his eyes at the ridiculous observation which, for whatever reason, Lord Burnley either did not notice or chose to ignore. "Do you have any particular intentions for this Season?"

Sending a lazy glance towards Lord Burnley, Robert shrugged.

"If you mean to ask whether or not I intend to pursue one particular young lady with the thought of matrimony in mind, then I must tell you that you are mistaken to even *think* that I should care for such a thing," he stated, plainly. "I am here only to enjoy myself."

"I see."

Lord Burnley gave no comment in judgment of Robert's statement, but Robert felt it nonetheless, quite certain that Lord Burnley now thought less of him for being here solely for his own endeavors. He scowled. Lord Burnley might have decided that it was the right time for him to wed, but Robert had no intention of doing so whatsoever. Given his good character, given his standing and his title, there would be very few young ladies who would suit him, and Robert knew that it would take a significant effort not only to first identify such a young lady but also to then make certain that she would suit him completely. It was not something that he wanted to put his energy into at present. For the moment, Robert had every intention of simply dancing and conversing and mayhap even calling upon the young ladies of the *ton,* but that would be for his own enjoyment rather than out of any real consideration.

Besides which, he told himself, *given that the* ton *will, no doubt, remember all that you did last Season, there will be many young ladies seeking out your company which would make it all the more difficult to choose only one, should you have any inclination to do so!*

"And are you to attend Lord Newport's ball tomorrow evening?"

Being pulled from his thoughts was an irritating interruption and Robert let the long sigh fall from his lips without hesitation, sending it in Lord Burnley's direction who, much to Robert's frustration, did not even react to it.

"I am," Robert replied, grimacing. "Although I do hope that the other guests will not make too much of my arrival. I should not like to steal any attention away from Lord and Lady Newport."

Allowing himself a few moments of study, Robert looked back at Lord Burnley and waited to see if there was even a hint of awareness in his expression. Lord Burnley, however, merely shrugged one shoulder and turned his head away, making nothing at all of what Robert had told him. Gritting his teeth, Robert closed his eyes and tried to force out another long, calming breath. He did not need Lord Burnley to remember what he had done, nor to celebrate it. What was important was that the ladies of the *ton* recalled it, for then he would be more than certain to have their attention for the remainder of the Season – and that was precisely what Robert wanted. Their attention would elevate him in the eyes of the *ton*, would bring him into sharp relief against the other gentlemen who were enjoying the Season in London. He did not care what the gentlemen thought of him, he reminded himself, for their considerations were of no importance save for the fact that they might be able to invite him to various social occasions.

Robert's shoulders dropped and he opened his eyes. Coming to White's this evening had been a mistake. He ought to have made his way to some soiree or other, for he had many invitations already but, given that he had only arrived in London the day before, had thought it too early to make his entrance into society. That had been a mistake. The *ton* ought to know of his arrival just as soon as was possible, so that his name might begin to be whispered amongst them. He could not bear the idea that the pleasant notoriety he had experienced last Season might have faded already!

A small smile pulled at his lips as he considered this, his heart settling into a steady rhythm, free from frustration and upset now. Surely, it was not that he was not remembered by society, but rather that he had chosen the wrong place to make his entrance. The gentlemen of London would not make his return to society of any importance, given that they would be jealous and envious of his desirability in the eyes of the ladies of the *ton*, and therefore, he ought not to have expected such a thing from them! A quiet chuckle escaped his lips as Robert shook his head, passing one hand over his eyes for a moment. It had been a simple mistake and that mistake had brought him irritation and confusion – but that would soon be rectified, once he made his way into full London society.

"You appear to be in better spirits now, Lord Crampton."

Robert's brow lifted as he looked back at Lord Burnley, who was studying him with mild interest.

"I have just come to a realization," he answered, not wanting to go into a detailed explanation but at the same time, wanting to answer Lord Burnley's question. "I had hoped that I might have been greeted a little more warmly but, given my history, I realize now that I ought not to have expected it from a group of gentlemen."

Lord Burnley frowned.

"Your history?"

Robert's jaw tightened, wondering if it was truly that Lord Burnley did not know of what he spoke, or if he was saying such a thing simply to be a little irritating.

"You do not know?" he asked, his own brows drawing low over his eyes as he studied Lord Burnley's open expression. The man shook his head, his head tipping gently to one side in a questioning manner. "I am surprised. It was the talk of London!"

"Then I am certain you will be keen to inform me of it," Lord Burnley replied, his tone neither dull nor excited, making Robert's brow furrow all the more. "Was it something of significance?"

Robert gritted his teeth, finding it hard to believe that Lord Burnley, clearly present at last year's Season, did not know of what he spoke. For a moment, he thought he would not inform the fellow about it, given that he did not appear to be truly interested in what they spoke of, but then his pride won out and he began to explain.

"Are you acquainted with Lady Charlotte Fortescue?" he asked, seeing Lord Burnley shake his head. "She is the daughter of the Duke of Strathaven. Last Season, when I had only just stepped into the title of the Earl of Crampton, I discovered her being pulled away through Lord Kingsley's gardens by a most uncouth gentleman and, of course, in coming to her rescue, I struck the fellow a blow that had him knocked unconscious." His chin lifted slightly as he recalled that moment, remembering how Lady Charlotte had practically collapsed into his arms in the moments after he had struck the despicable Viscount Forthside and knocked him to the ground. Her father, the Duke of Strathaven, had been in search of his daughter and had found them both only a few minutes later, quickly followed by the Duchess of Strathaven. In fact, a small group of gentlemen and ladies had appeared in the gardens and had applauded him for his rescue – and news of it had quickly spread through London society. The Duke of Strathaven had been effusive in his appreciation and thankfulness for Robert's actions and Robert had reveled in it, finding that his newfound status within the *ton* was something to be enjoyed. He had assumed that it would continue into this Season and had told himself that, once he was at a ball or soiree with the ladies of the *ton*, his exaltation would continue. "The Duke and Duchess were, of course, very grateful," he finished, as Lord Burnley nodded slowly, although there was no exclamation of surprise on his lips nor a gasp of astonishment. "The gentlemen of London are likely a little envious of me, of course, but that is to be expected."

Much to his astonishment, Lord Burnley broke out into laughter at this statement, his eyes crinkling and his hand lifting his still-full glass towards Robert.

"Indeed, I am certain they are," he replied, his words filled with a sarcasm that could not be missed. "Good evening, Lord Crampton. I shall go now and tell the other gentlemen here in White's precisely who you are and what you have done. No doubt they shall come to speak to you at once, given your great and esteemed situation."

Robert set his jaw, his eyes a little narrowed as he watched Lord Burnley step away, all too aware of the man's cynicism. *It does not matter,* he told himself, firmly. *Lord Burnley, too, will be a little jealous of your success, and your standing in the* ton. *What else should you expect other than sarcasm and rebuttal?*

Rising to his feet, Robert set his shoulders and, with his head held high, made his way from White's, trying to ignore the niggle of doubt that entered his mind. Tomorrow, he told himself, he would find things much more improved. He would go to whatever occasion he wished and would find himself, of course, just as he had been last Season – practically revered by all those around him.

He could hardly wait.

Check out the rest of the story in the Kindle store. More Than a Companion

JOIN MY MAILING LIST

Sign up for my newsletter to stay up to date on new releases, contests, giveaways, freebies, and deals!

Free book with signup!

Facebook Giveaways! Books and Amazon gift cards! Join me on Facebook: https://www.facebook.com/rosepearsonauthor

Website: www.RosePearsonAuthor.com

Follow me on Goodreads: Author Page

You can also follow me on Bookbub! Click on the picture below – see the Follow button?

212 | JOIN MY MAILING LIST

Printed in Dunstable, United Kingdom